ALSO BY LIZ ALDEN

<u>The Love and Wanderlust Series</u>

The Night in Lover's Bay (free prequel short story)

The Fling in Panama

The Slow Burn in Polynesia

The Second Chance in the Mediterranean

The Rival in South Africa (standalone novella)

The Player in New Zealand

The Best Friend in Indonesia (free standalone short story)

<u>Aged Like Fine Wine Series</u>

Rosé with My Fake Fiancé

Riesling with My Roommate

Prosecco with My Professor

Cava with My Colleague

<u>Winter Wanderlust Series</u>

Nutcracker with Benefits

Frosty Proximity

Ghost of Ex-mas Past

<u>Wanderlust Resort Series</u>

Beach Boss (free standalone short story)

Beach Resolution

Put it in Beach Mode

<u>Farm 2 Forking (a shared universe series)</u>

Butter You Up

<u>Standalones</u>

The Boudoir Arrangement

PROSECCO WITH MY PROFESSOR

A SWEET AND SPICY ROMANTIC COMEDY

AGED LIKE FINE WINE
BOOK 3

LIZ ALDEN

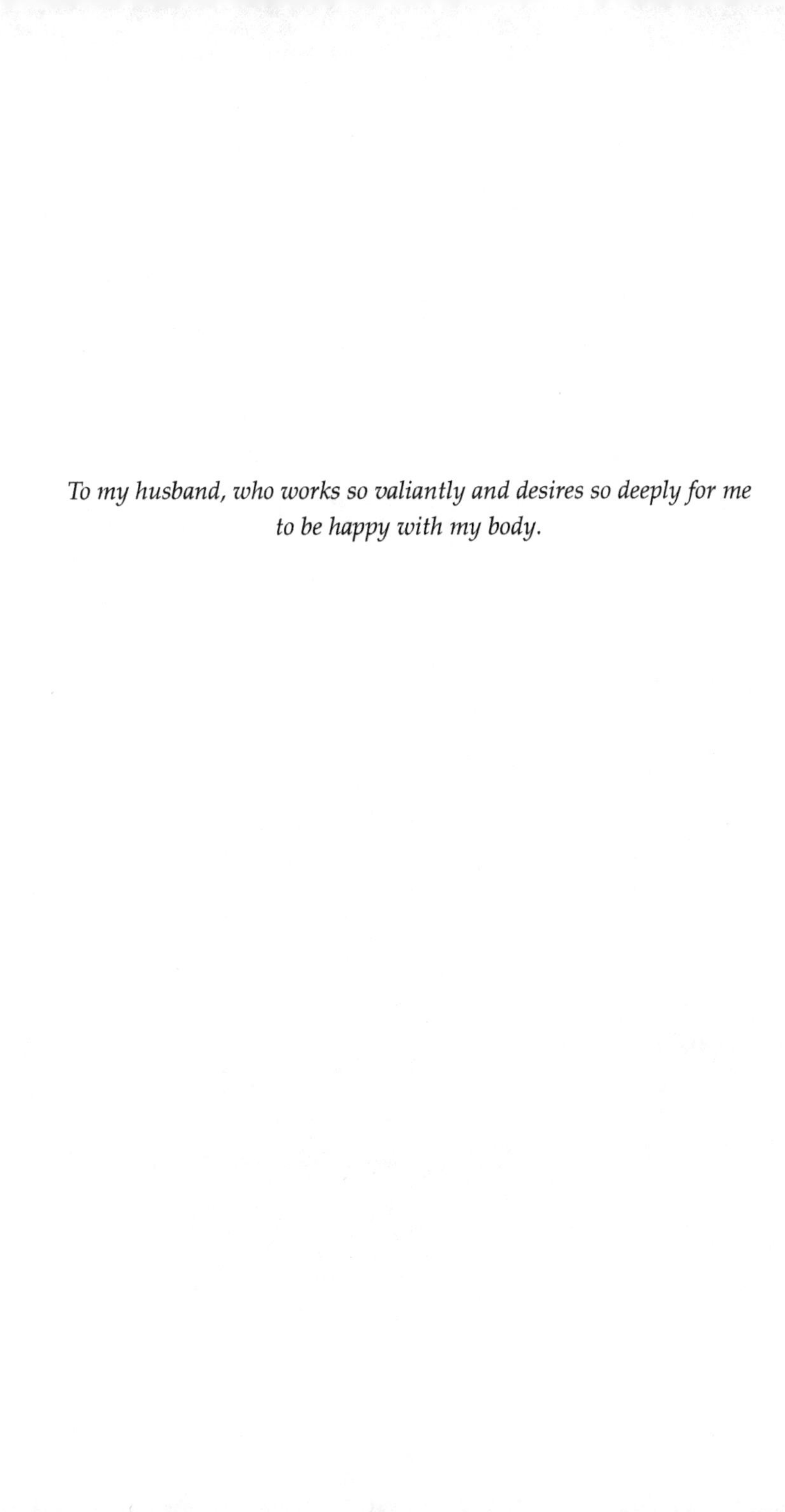

To my husband, who works so valiantly and desires so deeply for me to be happy with my body.

TO CONCERNED READERS

This book includes a female main character with body insecurities. It also includes a power imbalance between two mature characters.

As usual with my books, there are multiple graphic sex scenes. This one explores anal play and use of toys.

1

Emma

"Two Franciacorta, one Chianti, and one Prosecco," the bartender says as he puts four wine glasses in front of me, and thank god, it was a repeat order from before. I barely know any of those words; before coming to Europe, my wine selection typically consisted of red, white, or "champagne," which was definitely not champagne.

Not that I have had any champagne since moving here or that I know what the differences are, but still. I guess at forty-two years old, it's about time I broadened my horizons, so maybe buying some actual champagne should be on my to-do list.

"Grazie," I say, wincing because it doesn't sound as sexy on my tongue as it does his.

I thought it was a joke or inaccurate that Italian men are sexier, but in the brief time that I've been in Rome, I think that's true.

It must be the heady combination of the accent, the dark hair and olive skin, and the way they dress. The same was true with Spanish men in Madrid, where I just spent a month living with one of my best friends.

Speaking of Jade, she sidles up next to me at the bar, her long hair up in a ponytail that swings against my elbow. "Let me help." She grabs two glasses with one hand while I grab the other two. With her free hand on my elbow, she turns us back to our table where our other best friends, Sara and Tessa, sit.

I make a point *not* to look at the older man who smiled at me a few minutes ago.

Jade, however, is like a mind reader, especially with anything sex-related. She leans in with a whisper. "You have your eye on the silver fox down at the end of the bar?"

I glance over my shoulder to find him watching me, so I quickly snap my head forward again. This man is the perfect example of how stylish Italian men can be. The wavy, thick hair on the top of his head and his dark beard are salt-and-pepper and groomed. He's wearing a fitted navy blazer, but I lack the sartorial knowledge to describe why it looks so damn good on him, whereas my ex in a navy blazer looked like a country club dweeb.

Movement catches my gaze, and I glance over to find Jade wriggling her fingers at the silver fox.

I push her hand down as we arrive at the table. "Stop encouraging him," I hiss.

"Why?" Jade's smile turns from slightly flirty to fond as she looks at me.

"You're giving him false hope," I say.

"Honey, men are going to always hope to sleep with you." Jade, the shortest of us, huffs as she climbs onto the chair at our high-top table. She's five-four, with bronze skin and long dark hair that has a white streak in it. "You're beautiful and charming. Hope isn't something you give them; they already have it. And any guy worth going home with is going to know that having a conversation or flirtation with you is not a consolation prize. A man should be so honored."

I blush and glance at the man again. "It's not that I don't want to sleep with someone." I lean in and drop my voice to a whisper. "It's just that it's been so long. It feels like...like being revirginized."

"That's definitely not a thing," Jade interjects, pointing a finger at me. Sara and Tessa sip their wine, amused. The four of us have been best friends for ages. We met at Sara's yoga classes and then started going out for a drink afterward and our friendships blossomed from there. With Jade and I having lived together for the past month, we've become even closer, which is humorous since the two of us are opposites, at least when it comes to relationships.

"I know, I know. You've made us all read the book, Jade." The book on women's sexuality that Jade gave each of us a few years ago debunked a lot of myths and taught me way more about sex than twenty-three years of marriage did. Living with Jade taught me even more. I've only just started thinking about dating again, and she helped me think through some of my anxieties–what if a woman I was interested in wasn't queer, or what if a man was put off by my height.

It also made me a little sad. Like I was missing out on something I hadn't known was possible. Because while my marriage lasted for twenty-three years, my sex life with my husband didn't.

But I'm here in Rome, about to start an International MBA program, turning over a new leaf. Why shouldn't that extend to my sex life, too?

"I'm just saying," Jade points out, "that you have us all here. If you want to go talk to that guy, we can have, like, a signal. An eye roll if we need to rescue you from the conversation, or a wink if you're going to go home with him."

"And then we can make sure we have his information,"

Sara says, "just like y'all did with my roommate. And if anything goes wrong, we can help you." She recently moved in with a total stranger, but it's been almost a month now, and it is going well.

Jade blinks at Sara, possibly surprised that she's agreeing with her.

"But only if you're comfortable with it," Sara adds. Her hair, dark brown with a few gray hairs—unlike my completely gray hair—is up in a ponytail, and she's wearing a chic dress that shows off her yoga-toned body.

"Thanks, Sara," I say, but Jade hasn't taken her eyes off Sara.

"Hang on," Jade says, and now Sara has the full brunt of her attention. "Sara's been awfully relaxed this weekend." Jade twists her mouth to the side and wiggles an eyebrow. "Are you getting some frustration out somehow?"

"No!" Sara protests. "I am not sleeping with my roommate."

"Wow," Tessa says, leaning her elbow on the table and propping her chin in her hand, mirroring Jade. Her light blonde hair perfectly frames her face and real diamond earrings sparkle in the low light of the bar. "Jade didn't say anything about your roommate."

"That's not… I just meant…"

I can't help it; a giggle slips out, and I clap my hand over my mouth before it becomes a full-on laugh.

"You!" Sara says, pointing at me. "Go talk to him!" She jabs her thumb over her shoulder, and I groan.

I throw a pout at her, but then look over her shoulder. The man is still standing there. He's sipping from a rotund glass of red wine, listening to his friend, and as he swallows, his prominent Adam's apple visible, his eyes catch mine.

He smiles, and it's slow, like molasses. It's got a hint of a smirk to it and no teeth. This man is confident, like he knows he can give me an actual, honest-to-god, non-vibrator-triggered orgasm.

It's been at least a decade since I've had one of those.

"Okay." I draw in a breath and then take a sip of my Prosecco. "What do I say?"

"I always start with hi," Jade says helpfully, and I pinch her bicep. Jade yelps and rubs her arm but laughs as I stand, gather my courage, and walk toward the bar.

There's a space two seats down from the man I want to talk to, so I stand at it, giving myself a moment to think about what I'm going to say. The couple between us is like a protective barrier between me and the unknown.

I sip my wine, the bubbles dancing on my tongue. My friends have been encouraging me to get on dating apps, and I can see why: for an introvert like me, how on earth did we ever pick up people in bars?

"I thought you might be the Prosecco," a voice next to me says. It's deep, and the accent is there, but not thick. His voice rises and falls; the r of Prosecco rolls.

I turn, and it's him. The people between us have disappeared, and he stands a few feet away.

"Excuse me?" My cheeks warm. *He* said something to *me*.

"I heard your drink order," he says, stepping closer. "I thought, 'those women know their Italian wine', and then I tried to guess which was yours. And," he pauses, holding out a hand and tilting his head. "I was right."

I smile into my glass and take another sip. He's flirting. That's flirting, right? Maybe?

It's so subtle, and I'm used to Jade, who is an outrageous flirt and makes her intentions super clear from the start.

"Why did you think I was the Prosecco? Why not the Fran..."

"Franciacorta," he supplies, lip twitching.

Oof, I like the way he says that. "Yes. That one. Or the key..."

"Chianti."

"Chianti," I echo. I might keep naming wines over and over to hear him repeat the words back.

"Have you not seen the Hannibal Lecter movie?"

"No, because," I dramatically shudder, "A, I don't do horror movies, and B, that movie came out when I was probably…nine?" I guess. "Hardly appropriate for a child."

"I saw it when it came out. I was twenty-three, and I still don't think it was age-appropriate," he says, and I chuckle. "To answer your question, I thought you were the Prosecco because you looked like light. Like bubbles."

My cheeks heat. "Well, I'm not a bubbly person. Sorry to disappoint."

His lips roll inward, and he gives a small shake of his head. "Bubbles are not bubbly or shy; they just *are*. I wouldn't dream of trying to push the whimsies of men on something so beautiful." His gaze on me is pointed.

Words escape me. Is this real?

Another point in the favor of Italian men because I can't picture any of the American men I know back home as having the ability to pull a compliment like that off. I can't picture them even using the phrase *whimsies of men*. Maybe I just know the wrong men.

I realize my mouth is slightly open, and I've been staring. With a click, I close my jaw and extend my hand. "I'm Emma."

He takes my hand in his, and it's not over-the-top; there's no kissing of the knuckles or anything so flamboyant, but the handshake is firm and warm—like I'm in expert hands now. It sends a shiver up my spine.

"Santo," he says.

2

Santo

Emma is nervous, and when I glance over at the table of her friends, they quickly look away. "A girls' weekend?" I guess, lifting an eyebrow.

"Yes," she says, almost into her glass as she takes another sip. Emma is as tall as I am, and she's wearing flats, so we're perfectly eye-to-eye.

"Tell me, what do a bunch of beautiful women do in the city on a girls' weekend?"

It takes some prodding and follow-up questions, but eventually, we find our way. Emma tells me about her exploration of my city with her friends—food, walking cobblestone streets, hitting all the highlights like the Vatican and Trevi fountain. She has an American accent with a slight twang, one I can't place.

She loves it here, and when I tell her I've lived here most of my life, she begs me for recommendations.

"We have one last day together tomorrow. You must have some suggestions."

I pull my phone out of my pocket and open it, swiping

away texts from Vincente, my friend I was here with, that tell me he's left the bar already. "Where are you staying?"

"Just a few blocks from here, actually. But we are sharing hotel rooms." She blushes prettily, embarrassed, perhaps because she's making assumptions about where tonight is leading.

"I am not far from here either," I say, holding her gaze over the rim of my wineglass as I sip. "Plenty of privacy." Privacy, but not ideal on account of all the boxes that are stacked up for the impending move. But the bed's still there, made up for a few more nights of sleep.

Her blush deepens. Emma has fair skin, very faint lines at the edges of her brown eyes, and thick, long gray hair. I set my wineglass down, and she leans in as I show her a map and some suggestions on my phone for places to eat.

We talk about the options, complicated by one of her friends who is vegan, but we eventually settle on a quiet place I've been to a few times with a courtyard. I send it to her via Airdrop when she pulls out her phone.

From then on, I keep it light. She's clearly here for the weekend, and while she's shy, she's definitely not looking for anything long term—which is perfect for me.

I'm not looking for a third wife.

I'm just looking for a bit of fun.

When we order another round, I ask for water, too, and I make sure Emma hydrates between the wine. Her cheeks are still flushed, but from the wine or the attention, I'm not sure.

I've put my usual moves on her; a soft brush of her arm, a light touch on her back. When we clink glasses, I don't step back out of her space.

She's got big, beautiful eyes I could get lost in for the night and a small delicate mouth that I want to touch. That ache of desire has a hold of me, and I want to take her home.

Based on the way her eyes drop down to my mouth, I think she has the same idea too. I lean in closer, and her lips part at my nearness. Her eyelids flutter as I press a gentle kiss to the corner of her mouth. When I pull back just enough to breathe, she turns slightly, lining us up. I press another kiss to her lips, and she softens against me.

"Emma," I say when I pull away. "Come home with me?"

Her teeth capture her bottom lip and worry it as her eyes bounce between mine, but she nods, the unbitten side of her lip tipping up into a smile.

I signal for the bill and Emma finishes her glass of water while she waits and then leads me toward her friends. They're already watching us and grinning; the short, long-haired one looking smug.

Emma says something to them in a whisper before I catch up to her, and one of the women, the brunette, claps her hand over her mouth, eyes dancing in amusement. Emma picks up a purse from the empty chair.

"Hello," I tell them.

Before I can say anything else, the brunette drops her hand and clears her throat. "Can I see some ID, please?"

The woman with the gray streak in her hair guffaws. I pull out my ID, and the brunette takes a picture of it.

"Where are you going?"

I give her my address.

"Are you driving?"

"Okay, Mama Bear," the gray-streak woman interrupts.

"It's okay," I say. "We will take an Uber." I would take a taxi if I was by myself—well, actually, I would walk, but in the name of efficiency, a car would be best—but I want Emma's friends to know she's safe, and Uber gives them the ability to track the ride.

"That she'll order and let us track," she answers primly.

Exactly what I had in mind. "Yes, signora. I will take excellent care of her."

That mollifies the protective one. Emma tugs me away

when the other whistles, blowing them a kiss as we walk toward the exit and calling goodbye.

Out on the street, Emma covers her hand with her face. "Oh my god," she mumbles.

"What?" I ask, bending down to see her better, but I'm pretty sure she's laughing.

"Is it always this embarrassing?"

I gently tug one wrist, and she drops it. I keep my grip on it and use it to pull her closer. Those rosy pink cheeks haven't faded at all. "What is embarrassing about it?" I ask, but don't let her answer. "It's life," I say with a shrug and grab her other hand too. "It's a *good* life."

"Good, huh?" she says. We're closer now, the September night air between us is almost chilly. She bites her lip, gazing at me.

I wrap my arms around her, taking her hands with me behind her back. Her chest presses against mine, her breath hitting my lips and her eyes widening. Our noses touch, just a small nudge at first before I purposefully drag the tip of mine across hers. Her eyelashes flutter, the smell of wine and sweet botanicals wrapping around us.

I close the last millimeter, brushing my lips against her bottom one, just a tiny drag of soft skin against soft skin. I nip, and it startles her.

Her lips part, and I go in for a full kiss, my lips easing hers open and my arms pulling her harder against me. Emma lets me keep the lead, but she responds eagerly, with a sweet little moan in the back of her throat as I barely dip my tongue in.

I pull back before we get too heated. "Emma, call the Uber." I give her my address while she orders the car, and then I cup her head with my hands, fusing our mouths together again. These kisses are hotter, more insistent, and Emma kisses back with more confidence.

A car honks, and I ease back, releasing my grip and

steadying her when she sways slightly. I open the door to our ride and guide her in, following right behind.

To my relief, Emma doesn't scoot all the way over. When the door slams behind me, I pull her toward me and cover my mouth with hers again. She grips the lapels of my jacket, keeping me close, as if afraid that I'll pull away.

What would be a long, cobble-stoned walk down dark streets is a brief car ride. We get out at our destination, and I thank the driver.

When I turn back to Emma, she's laughing to herself.

"What?" I ask.

She presses her hands to her cheeks. "I haven't really done that before." At my look, she laughs again. "Making out in front of a stranger, I mean."

"Did you *like* it?" How much did she like it?

She tilts her head as I usher her through the vestibule and into the lobby. "Are you asking if I am an exhibitionist?"

I press her up against the wall of the lobby and kiss her, this time deep with more tongue. When she's thoroughly disheveled, I trace light kisses up the side of her face. "I just want to know what you like," I whisper in her ear.

"You," she says back, shyly.

Fuck, that's hot. I grunt and thrust my hips against her, watching as her eyelids flutter in arousal. Pushing off from the wall, I lead her up the stairs and into my apartment. My cat, Zola, has been acting out lately, the boxes and luggage clueing her into the impending move. I brace myself walking in and hope that she hasn't made her displeasure known again with a mess, but everything looks in order and, most importantly, smells good.

Emma will be the last woman to come back to this apartment that I've lived in for six years. I'm downgrading again. My previous home was more befitting a CFO's salary. This one was better on a professor's salary but still enormous. The new apartment will be better suited to a lone professor and his cat.

The entryway is small, and Emma looks around. When she turns her attention back to me, her back is against the wall. She's still flushed, lips kiss-swollen.

My eyes travel down her body. Full breasts, soft belly, generous hips and thighs, all wrapped in a subdued purple dress that ends at the knee. It's a modest outfit but curve-hugging.

And also provides easy access.

I let my finger trace the same path my eyes took. She sucks in a little when I pass her stomach, but I ignore that. I'll prove to her how sexy her body is.

When I can't reach any further, I draw my gaze back up to hers and hold it for a beat before slowly lowering myself to my knees. Years of playing football means I can't do this for long, but a few minutes will be completely worth the stiffness.

Emma's eyes widen.

My fingers are at the hem of her dress, playing with it lightly. I inch it up the soft expanse of pale thigh, keeping my eyes on hers. Her breath accelerates, her lips part, and the smell of her arousal hits me. My eyelids flutter, and I nuzzle the skin I've exposed.

When I look up, Emma's dropped her head back and I take it as an invitation to move further. I groan when I reveal her soft pink panties with a damp spot between her legs.

"So sexy." I whisper the words against her skin. Her hips shift as I run my fingers up her sides, hooking them into her panties and tugging down. Her stance widens, so I only take them down to her knees.

She smells so fucking good. Emma's left her hair natural, soft curls in such a light, fine color, that I can't tell if it's blonde or gray. I place my palm on her belly, using my thumb to stroke the hairs. When I glance up to check on her, she's thrown her head back, her chest heaving in anticipation.

I press my open mouth against her at the bottom of her mons. My tongue slides down, spread flat and delving between her lips and over her clit, curling when I get to—

"Stop," Emma says, and I freeze. I pull back to look up at her, and my stomach twists. She's not wide-eyed in pleasure but in panic. "I have to—" She fumbles with her panties. "I have to go."

"What? Emma—"

She doesn't even get the material up over her hips, just enough so that she can leave. The next thing I know, I'm on my knees in my empty hallway, the doors slamming behind her, leaving me alone.

"*Miao.*"

Correction—alone with my cat.

3

Emma

I'M NOT SURE WHAT I'M GOING TO WALK INTO AT THE HOTEL room—it hasn't been long, my friends could still be out at the bar—but when I open the door to one of the adjoining rooms we've booked, Sara is sitting on top of the covers of one bed and on her phone, a soft smile on her face. She glances up at me in surprise. "Hey, what are you doing back?"

I don't know where Jade and Tessa are, but I throw my bag in the general direction of the table and flop face-first onto the bed next to her. "I couldn't do it," I say, voice muffled by the comforter, but thankfully, Sara is proficient in Emma-feelings enough to make an educated guess. Her hand lands softly on my shoulder.

"Couldn't do what?"

I flop right-side-up and we both wiggle into a comfortable position on the bed, backs against the headboard.

"He wanted to go down on me. I mean, he went down on me. But it was..." I trail off, not sure how to finish the sentence.

"It wasn't good?" Sara guesses.

"I don't know," I admit. "Do you know how long it's been since a man has gone down on me?" Then I wince because Sara's husband passed many years ago when her daughter was a toddler. "Sorry. I should remember who I'm talking to."

"It's okay," Sara says, grabbing my hand and pulling it into her lap, then patting it. "How long has it been?"

I have to think about when the last time my ex-husband did that—I *try* to think about it, but I'm tired, and it was not that memorable. Maybe our twentieth anniversary? "I honestly don't remember the last time Bruce did that. Years. He never did like it, anyway."

Sara chuckles. "It's been a long time for me, too, so my memory might be a little hazy. But I don't remember Kit being all that good at it. I mean, we were so young; everything was just rolled up with enthusiasm. And after Zoe was born, it was a lot of quickies as we could catch them."

"What about some of the guys you've dated recently?"

"I think we either never got to that part or skipped the foreplay."

"You should never skip the foreplay," Jade interrupts as the door to the bathroom swings open. She's wrapped her hair up in a towel and has a T-shirt and shorts on for sleeping. "Emma," she says, eyebrow raising in surprise. "Is everything okay?"

By the time I've filled Jade in, the door to the hallway opens, and Tessa joins us. Before I can say anything, Jade waves a hand. "Yes, Emma's back. She's fine. He was fine, but the night was not a success."

"Oh," Tessa says, sitting at the foot of the bed and giving my bare foot a squeeze. "Are you going to see him again?"

I shake my head hard. "Definitely not. I basically just ran out of his apartment, and he probably thinks there's something wrong with me."

"Why did you run out?" Jade asks.

"Because it was embarrassing. I wasn't expecting that!"

"What?" Jade asks, her brow wrinkling.

"I wasn't expecting him to put his mouth down there! I just thought...I don't know! I couldn't stop thinking about how it had been a few hours since I'd showered and I had just peed at the bar and I haven't done any upkeep down there because obviously I wasn't planning to go home with a guy and..." Great, now I'm crying. "I guess I'm just not ready yet."

"Hey," Tessa coos. "That's okay. It's all taking steps and trying something new, right?"

"Emma, babe, I'm so sorry. I didn't mean to pressure you." Jade sucks her bottom lip into her mouth, the skin under her teeth turning white as she worries it.

"You didn't pressure me. Really. I was excited at the bar, but when he was actually...you know...I just couldn't turn my brain off and enjoy it."

"You definitely have to be in the right headspace for it," Tessa says. "A bit of confidence goes a long way."

I sit up, wiping my eyes, and give my friends my best attempt at a smile. "It gets better, right?"

"Of course it does!" Jade assures me.

Sara agrees, even though I think it's more wishful thinking than anything else.

But Tessa, the only one of us actually in a relationship, smiles knowingly and goes a little dreamy. She must be thinking about her boyfriend, Luc. Sara, Jade, and I exchange glances and then Jade lunges for the other bed, grabbing a pillow. Sara and I take the ones from behind us and whack Tessa.

She laughs and squeals, fending off the blows as best she can.

We don't pillow fight for long—seriously, a pillow fight at our age? Bruce, my ex, would have keeled over with a heart attack over me having a pillow fight with my "hot friends"— and end up all on the same bed, sprawled out and laughing.

Weapons down, Jade returns to the important topics. "It's a great sign that he went down on you, though. Like, I hate to say how low my bar has gotten lately. I'm fine with any foreplay, but goddamn, so many men want to skip right to p-in-v, and I'm fucking tired of it."

Tessa hums. "You know, the first time Luc went down on me, I asked if he wanted me to shower first. I get that we're all human and have bodily functions and whatnot. It's a legit concern, but some men just really like it. And then, once you get into it, you don't really think about anything else." She shrugs.

"Hard agree," Jade adds.

That's what I worry about. Sometimes, with Bruce, he gave up before I could come. It's so hard to stay present.

Plus, I'm pretty sure Jade and Tessa keep their pubic hair relatively trim. Maybe I should ask for some tips.

Tessa departs for the bathroom, and Jade and I vacate to the other bedroom. I shower, washing off any lingering smells of wine and hot Italian men, and then get in bed. Jade, in the other bed, flips over on her side to face me before I turn out the light.

"I'm sorry your night didn't work out," she says softly.

"I know. But it was a step forward, and I wouldn't have been brave enough for that without your support. Thanks for that."

"Any time, babe. And now you'll probably meet some cute fellow MBA student who's a few years younger than you but has all the eagerness and stamina that comes with it, and he can rock your world."

I chuckle at that. Luc is younger than Tessa, but I'm not sure that interests me. I like the maturity and self-assuredness Santo carried. Maybe there's someone like that waiting for me, and maybe he'll be in the crowd of new students.

———

IT'S A TEARY GOODBYE WITH MY BEST FRIENDS, BUT IT'S TEMPERED by the fact that I'll see them again in a month. After waving to the car that whisks them off to the airport, I take my things and call my own Uber to go to my new apartment.

I have two large bags with me from my time in Madrid and a small bag for the weekend. My intention was to leave the big bags packed until I got to my new place, but I made a huge mess looking for things in them—half of which I ended up finding in the smaller bag after a harried search—and I didn't pack them up as neatly anymore. Hence, I greet the landlord of the apartment complex with bulging bags I can barely carry, plus a handful of sweatshirts that mysteriously no longer fit in my suitcases.

The man is nice enough, showing me the small entrance with double doors, the (very European) cramped elevator where we stuff my bags in with us, and the small apartment that I'll be living in.

It's fully furnished, so by the time my bags are in and we've made a few trips down to the storage area to get the boxes I shipped over ahead of time, the space is feeling rather tiny. Plus, my apartment is one of the unrenovated ones in the building, which means it is cheaper. I think most of these are unfurnished and nicer. Since it's just me, I don't need a lot of space, but I wanted to be close to the school.

I'm not the only one moving in today—down the hallway there are boxes stacked outside of another door, and someone else is moving in on the first floor too.

"We house a lot of students and professors," my landlord explains. "Not...how do you say in English? Dormitory?"

"Dorm." I think back to the previous fall, moving my youngest child into their dorm room in LA. It's very different from these quiet halls and humble apartments.

"Yes. Next to you, there's a student at the fashion institute. The new one, down the hall"—he points in the general direction of the boxes—"is a professor. I think the same university as you?"

"That would be nice." I picture a female professor who might be closer to my age, someone who could become a mentor or even a friend.

He leaves me to unpack, and as I'm trying to decide where to store my shell suitcase, there's a knock at my new door.

There are voices in the hallway, but as I open my door, another one closes down the hall and there's only one person outside. Well, one person and a barking dog.

A young woman, about the age of my kids, I estimate, stands in the hallway with the dog on a leash. The dog is stout, with one of those scrunched-up noses. A French bull-dog, maybe? I'm not good with dog breeds.

"Oliver! Taci!" The woman glares down at the dog. When she looks back up, she brightens. "I am Eva. I live next door." She gestures down the hall toward the boxes. Eva has a thick Italian accent, short dark hair, and a nose piercing. She smells faintly of cigarette smoke. Oliver is still harrumphing at me.

"Emma," I offer her my hand, and we shake. "I hear you are a fashion student."

"Yes, I am." We chat for a few minutes until Oliver impatiently tugs at the leash to go back home. "Good luck with your studies," Eva says as she walks away, which seems like a very final thing to say to someone who you'll see every day, probably, but I chalk it up to a language barrier.

Back inside, I put a few more things away and check my phone. There are messages in the group text with my kids, who want to do a video call tonight and settled on nearly 10 p.m. my time. Also in the app are various "I'm home" messages from my friends, and I send them some pics of my apartment.

I fall asleep on the couch and wake up to darkness. Blinking in confusion, I sit up before looking out the window. Two golden, glowing eyes stare back at me.

I stifle a scream, my heart leaping in my throat, before I recognize that it's a cat. They slowly blink at me.

My apartment doesn't have a lot of windows, but there are two tall ones that face the building next door. They must have a ledge the cat is sitting on.

I stand, and the cat disappears before I can say or do anything else. I close the curtains anyway—no peeping toms, human or otherwise, are invited. Who lets their black cat roam freely at night?

4

Emma

I UNPACK AND TAKE SEVERAL TRIPS TO THE SUPERMARKET TO BUY all the things I need that I didn't want to pack: toiletries, cooking supplies, new sheets for the bed, a hair dryer. It's good to practice my conversational Italian—which I'm learning via an app—but also makes me very glad that the MBA program I'm enrolled in is taught in English.

My disastrous night with Santo is still pretty fresh in my mind, and I stare at the aisle of shaving creams, razors, and electrical implements that are, I'm guessing, by their packaging and color and some handy outlines on the back of the box, intended for women's landscaping.

If I'm going to consider dating again or even just meeting someone in my classes, maybe I need to sit down and consider what I want to do to maintain myself.

I would rather do some research than buy something spur-of-the-moment that goes to waste, so I check out with my normal toiletries and head back to my new place.

Once unpacked, I pick up my phone and text my friends for advice.

. . .

EMMA

Are y'all available for a phone call?

SARA

I am.

TESSA

Me too.

JADE

I'm out grocery shopping. The fridge is barren. Is this like a call-to-catch up or is this a level 5 emergency?

I TAKE A DEEP BREATH. IF I'M ACTUALLY GOING TO GO THROUGH with this, then I should get more comfortable *talking about it* with my favorite people in the world.

If I'm going to try dating, I type.

Delete, delete.

What do you do about your–

Delete, delete.

Ugh. I hate that these words aren't sexy or fun for me. I type out a third attempt and hit send with a cringe.

EMMA

I'm looking for um landscaping advice?

TWO SECONDS LATER, MY PHONE BUZZES WITH AN INCOMING video call from Jade. I answer, and the screen fills with her face, her cheeks flushed and hair bouncing as she power-walks.

"What happened to grocery shopping?"

"Yeah, well, I had just started, and all there was in the cart so far was wine, so I ditched it and am going home so I can give you one hundred percent of my focus. Plus, someone once told me it was extremely inappropriate to discuss our sex lives in the dairy section." Jade grins at me.

Me. Someone was me.

"I thought you were out of food?"

"Babe, I would rather eat plain spaghetti than miss this."

The screen swaps over and I see Tessa in her kitchen. We say hello and then Sara pops in. It looks like she's in the living room of Chris's house.

The view switches back to Jade. "Emma, tell. Us. Everything. What made you want to do some maintenance? Do you have a date?"

"No, but I will. Someday. And I want to be prepared."

"Is there something in particular you want to do with it?" Tessa asks.

"What do men like?"

"Oh my god, there's such a variety," Jade says. She blows out a breath.

"Well, in the past twenty-three years, it's only been Bruce, my gyno, and Santo."

"Did Santo say anything to you about it?"

"No."

"Were you worried about it?" Sara chimes in.

"Yes."

"Why?" That's Jade again.

"I guess...I was maybe worried about stray hairs? And I wanted him to like it. And I was worried it was too much... down there."

"Look," Jade says. "My experience is that if a man is going to *complain* about the hair on your pussy, he's going to find other things to complain about, too, things that aren't really any of his business. And those men are never the ones who maintain themselves, either. So, if he *does* say something negative about it: red flag."

"The point is to do what makes you comfortable," Tessa says.

"Yeah," I say, frustration edging my voice. "But I don't *know* what would make me comfortable. And what if I hate it?"

"It'll grow out," Jade says, reasonably. "You don't know how your skin will respond to a wax or a full shave, so I think your best bet, if you want to do anything at all, is to use an electric razor and trim the hair."

"It won't be prickly?"

"It might be at first," she muses. "But it depends how much hair you have. Also, hair can go a ways back, so keep an eye on that."

"What, like…all the way?"

Jade shrugs. "My waxer does all of that."

Someone going down on me wouldn't be able to see that…would they? It's not like I would ask for anything *back there*.

"I don't," Tessa says. "And Luc doesn't mind."

The three of us sigh. Luc doesn't mind *anything* about Tessa. I'm so glad she is with someone who appreciates her curves. It gives me hope that someone out there—aside from Bruce—will want to be with me despite my height and shape.

Well, I guess Santo doesn't mind it. He *did* take me home with him.

By the time my friends and I hang up, I've got a solid plan to trim everything tonight. I already have an electric waterproof razor, so I take it in the shower with me, turning the water as hot as it will go.

After washing my hair, the shower stall is full of steam, and I'm pleasantly relaxed from the heat. I squirt shaving cream onto my palm and lather up. The hair between my legs is coarse, so I run the electric razor against my skin in small strokes, rinsing frequently. It's awkward, bending over to see myself, pulling my skin this way and that to do a thorough job.

One time, Jade took the four of us to an art museum that had an erotic art exhibit. At the entrance, taking up an entire wall, were plaster casts of vulvas. There must have been at least a hundred, and I remember being shocked at the range and diversity. I couldn't help but think that some were more pretty than others, even though I know that society has trained me to look at women's bodies from a male gaze.

With Bruce, we never talked about my body like that. I have no idea if he thought mine was pretty.

Do I? Does Santo?

The back is even more awkward, more feeling by hand than being able to see anything. I think I do a good job, though.

Satisfied, I turn the razor off and put it on the hanging rack. I pick the shower head out of the holder and point the stream between my legs, rubbing with my hands to make sure I get any loose hairs and shaving cream off.

I stroke my hand over my mound, from top to bottom. It's not smooth like when I shave my legs and the skin is soft and hairless, but I think I like it.

I also like the way the warm water feels, and my stroking hands turn more purposeful.

Leaning against the wall, I let my fingers slip between my folds. I've never been one of those women who was into shower heads—there isn't enough friction and pressure for me—but the combination of my hand and the warm water turns me on.

I pull up the memory of Santo on his knees in front of me from just a few nights ago.

I was so surprised, but the hot, wet kisses he left on my

inner thigh made my stomach flip in a delicious way. Even thinking about it makes my stomach flip now. I run a finger up my inner lips and circle my clit, repeating the movement again and again. With my fingers wet, it almost feels like a tongue.

Soon I need more, so I take two fingers and press harder every time I circle my clit. My thighs tense, and my core tugs, urging me to press harder, circle faster, focus on that spot that needs attention, and I'm getting close…I let out a small moan.

On the other side of the wall, Oliver barks.

It startles me so badly that I drop the shower head, which goes crazy in the bottom of the shower stall. I catch it and put it up to the sounds of Eva shouting at her dog. "Oliver! Taci!"

Great, the neighbor I *just met* has now heard me masturbating. I turn off the shower.

Can this week get any worse?

5

Santo

IT'S BEEN A BUSY WEEK SINCE EMMA RAN OUT ON ME. ASIDE from Zola somehow escaping my apartment once, the new living arrangements are working out well. I've met my new neighbor, Eva, and her dog Oliver. Vincente has been over to see the place, and tonight we are out for night-before-the-first-day-of-program drinks.

Unlike last week, I am not inspired to take anyone home. Perhaps it is that we spent too much time talking about the upcoming year of teaching or that my mind is elsewhere with the move, but I didn't encounter anyone that interested me. Even Vincente hasn't let his eyes wander much. He's married but still has opinions, and sometimes I think he's more interested in my sex life than his own, which he calls "playing by the rules."

But now, our conversation centers on the upcoming year. As one of the more senior faculty members of our university, I have a better chance of choosing my work. All of the faculty are busy as hell, but I get to pick my courses, and Vincente, a decade my junior, has less influence over what he works on.

"It's a perfect topic," he rants. "Gamification and environmentalism are both hot right now. I can't believe the director isn't going to add it to the curriculum."

I grunt in sympathy. Our university has a new director managing the full-time MBA program, and there's been a bit of upheaval over it. Our previous director stepped down because of health issues, or at least that's the story. Unlike the previous two directors, he is not staying on as a professor, which makes me believe that the split was less amicable than the university presented.

"Director Greco hasn't approached you about making any changes, has he?"

I shake my head. This year, I'm already taking on more than I would like. I have one full-time MBA and two undergraduate courses per term, and I'm expected to turn in one new case study a year in addition to publishing a book. And don't forget about the consulting work.

For a man with a net worth in the eight figures, I shouldn't be so busy. But outside of the university, I only have my cat and my ex-stepdaughter. My mother died a few years ago, my father before that, and I never had children of my own. Leaving the tech industry for academia wiped the slate clean, as most of my friends didn't have time for someone they couldn't network with.

It was a rude awakening, but I probably would have done the same thing.

"How do you think he's doing, anyway?" Vincente asks. He flags the bartender down for another beer.

"The new director?" He nods. "He doesn't have a straightforward job."

Vincente laughs. "That is an understatement. I can't imagine having to lead experts in leadership. It must feel like everyone's looking over your shoulder all the time."

Kind of like the expectations everyone has when they hear my last name.

"No one's happy with an outside hire," I add. "Especially not one with such a history of fundraising."

Vincente makes a face of disgust. Even among a group of academics that understand the bottom line, no one enjoys fundraising. "You teach Change Management; surely you have some thoughts."

I point at Vincente. "See. Exactly that."

Vincente laughs, and I get away with that non-answer, and the conversation moves on to something else.

Back in my new apartment hours later, I prepare for bed. Zola sits in a wooden bowl I have on the table reserved for her. She never sits in it just right, her weight off to one side enough that I worry she's going to tip the bowl over, but she never does. At least, not this bowl, anyway.

There's also a pinecone in it. She refuses to sit in the bowl if I take the pinecone out.

I flop onto the mattress. At some point Zola will move to the bed with me, but for now, she's happy with the bowl and pinecone, so I figure I'll have some "alone time." I rest my hand on my dick over the black briefs.

My mind drifts back, as it has often this past week, to Emma.

I don't know why Emma ran out, and I've played it over and over in my mind since then. I made sure she felt safe, her friends knew where she was, she'd found the making out in the car hot, her kisses and the taste of her pussy were all signaling to me that she had been enjoying herself.

In my sex life, I've always found that things are never straightforward and simple, but I am frustrated that Emma just ran without talking about it. Bottling things up does not make for satisfying sex.

Perhaps it's best then. I couldn't be that for her, somehow, and besides, she's gone back to the States, and I'll never see her again.

That doesn't mean I can't think about it, though. I

remember getting to my knees in front of Emma and allow myself to think about how that would have played out; using my lips, tongue, and teeth on her until she shoved her hands into my hair and ground onto my face. Or maybe she'd come fast, desperate for me.

My dick hardens, and I shove the waistband down, taking a firm grip. I close my eyes and stroke, thinking about fucking her right there in the hallway after she's come, or walking her back to my bed. How would I have fucked her? I don't know why she ran away, but I hope she would want something other than lights off and under-the-covers sex. Maybe she'd—

On the other side of the wall, a raucous barking starts up, so loud it makes me jump, my hand leaving my dick as if guilty of something.

"Oliver! Shut up!" Eva shouts, loud enough to be heard over the barks. "God damnit!"

I've heard Oliver a few times through the wall; usually, he barks when someone's at her door, but he quiets down quickly. Eva, I almost never hear, though she has a loud voice. It's not as loud as Oliver, apparently. I wait until all is quiet and then start up again, keeping my mouth shut because while Oliver is loud, I don't want to risk my neighbor hearing me.

But not thirty seconds later, Oliver barks again, and I have to listen to Eva repeat her admonishments.

I stroke myself again, much quieter this time, nearly holding my breath. A few strokes in, Oliver barks. I sit up, gesturing wildly to the empty room. I'm not making any noise, but somehow, Oliver is barking at me. I live next door to a masturbation detection alarm with four legs and super-sonic hearing.

There goes my sex life.

———

My father would hate this, I think as I walk into the university building on Monday. It's fairly unremarkable from the outside; a tan brick front that looks much like any other building in the district of Borgo, but inside houses one of the best International MBA programs in the world.

That wouldn't have mattered to him, though.

Offredi men don't teach; they do!

We don't work for other people.

When I was your age…

That one almost stops me in my tracks. Because in two years, that sentence will end with "…I was dead."

I heard my dad start that sentence plenty of times. *When I was your age, I was putting food on the table by going door to door. When I was your age, I made my first million. When I was your age…*

Dad had always wanted me to take the same path that he had. He wanted me to start as he did, with nothing in my pockets, and he did the best he could to make that a reality. I was supposed to make my own path, and when it was easier for me than it had been for him—at first—that had made him angry.

The Offredi name took me far in life because when people heard it, doors opened. Maybe they thought I would lead them to my dad. So, despite Dad trying his hardest, I was never short of opportunities. Teaching business to young, wide-eyed students is one of them, and although my father would hate having a son who is a lowly professor, I take a deep satisfaction in knowing that it was my—our—last name that got me the job.

And now, instead of refusing to help the next generation, I have helped hundreds of MBA students elevate their careers and success. Where my dad refused to reach down and lend a hand, I am building stairs.

I trot up the stairs to the first floor where my office is.

Technically, it's not the first day of the program, as courses won't formally start for two weeks, but there is a week reserved for orientation and then a week to discuss current events' impact on business. I'll be attending a few sessions plus meetings within my department.

I've already been over the curriculum and the schedule, and there's not much for me to do but show my face today.

My office is small—a long line in a hallway of equally small offices. I say hello to a few colleagues and give polite head nods to the few that are new. When I get to my office, I close the door behind me, set my bag down on the desk, and slump into my seat.

I didn't expect the walk in to dredge up so many thoughts about my father. Even decades after his death, he still lingers like a specter in my life.

If Dad was still alive, what would I say? What would he say?

There's nothing like the death of a loved one to make you realize how little you knew them. I thought—hoped, maybe— that someday there would be a reconciliation between us. That someday I'd work for him, alongside him, after having made my own way. After I'd made him proud, I guess.

Instead, he died suddenly, an aneurism when he was fifty-eight. Not that fifty-eight is terribly young—I snort at the thought—but Dad had still been at the top of his game.

And his will had been a shock. Two silent investors I hadn't known existed had the first right of refusal to buy his shares in the import company he'd built. The rest of his assets —namely, money—went to me, his only recognized child and the man he'd told to make his own way his entire life.

I didn't know what to make of that. He didn't want me to have the business, but he gave me all his money when he'd refused to seed my first startup, when he'd refused to pay for my college, when he'd refused…

Well, regardless, here I am about to teach the basics of business to the bright minds of the future.

There's a knock on the door and at my curt, "yes," it swings open to reveal Vincente. "Hey, feeling good for the first day?"

I shed my thoughts and shake Vincente's hand. "Ready to teach Business Analytics to a bunch of twenty-year-olds?" I ask, naming my first course of the year that'll start in two weeks. "Absolutely."

"Not quite Organizational Behaviors," he teases, naming his own course, "so I'm sure you can handle it."

I walk back around my desk and pull a few things out of my bag that I don't need before I sling it over my shoulder.

"Wait," Vincente says. "You've been attacked."

My brow wrinkles in confusion, and he gestures at my gray sleeve. I twist my arm and see a collection of short, black hairs on the back of my elbow, where it's hard for me to see.

"Zola got you again."

"Shit. How does she always know exactly where to sit so that I can't see it? I swear to god I left my jacket on the bed for thirty seconds."

"She's the devil," Vincente points out. Zola hates him, but he's also not a cat person.

We take a few minutes to get my jacket off and give the sleeve a vigorous rubbing. "I need to bring a lint roller and stash it in my drawer," I grumble.

"Or get rid of the cat."

"No wonder she hates you."

"She hates everyone."

Dressed once again, we make our way out to the hallway, and I close my door behind us. "She likes me."

He eyes me skeptically. Just before we moved to the new apartment, Zola made her displeasure well-known, and I had a few angry scratches on my arms. Even before that, she hid when anyone came over. She's always been like that, ever since I adopted her. But in the new place, her anger lurks in the living spaces even when she doesn't. I'd forgotten how bad the wrath of Zola can be.

"She needs to get used to her new space," I say for the fifteenth time in a few days. "She'll be fine."

6

____

Emma

IT'S A TEN-MINUTE WALK FROM MY APARTMENT TO THE university where I'll be getting my first—and hopefully only —postgraduate education. I walked by the building two days ago, just scoping the place out, figuring out where to get a cup of coffee or grab lunch during my breaks.

I still can't believe I get to live in Rome, much less get my MBA.

It's relatively early and I want to be well-caffeinated for my first day in classes, so I stop at the coffee shop near my apartment to pick up a cup.

I haven't quite figured this out yet. Last time I ordered un caffè and got an espresso, which is a little intense for me. I hang back a bit to eavesdrop on other people's orders—a tip Tessa gave me—and figure out how to get something closer to my regular order at the coffee shop back home.

After a few minutes, though, I give up and order a caffè freddo off the menu. I wait for it at the counter after fumbling with my bad Italian and thanking the barista in English.

The guy next to me catches my eye.

"American, yes?" He's in his twenties, possibly, with deeply tanned skin and a floppy haircut. His smile is friendly.

I nod.

"What is your name?"

"Emma," I say.

He steps close. Too close. "You American women like Italians, no?"

"Uh…"

His grin shifts, and it's not so friendly anymore.

This isn't the first time in my few days here that I've encountered unwanted attention, but this is definitely the most forward one.

"Emma, che bella che sei. I can help you, you know."

My drink appears like magic, and I grab it. The southerner in me politely grits my teeth and says goodbye while walking away.

I make it out the door but move faster when he calls my name outside the shop. I take the next left turn, even though I'm not sure it's the correct direction.

Keeping the pace up for a few minutes, I try to shake the encounter off. I've been catcalled once already. It was with my friends, and maybe the guy wasn't catcalling me specifically, but it was enough that we stood closer together walking to the Pantheon.

I pull out my phone and figure out how to get to class, glad I got up early enough on the first day to account for some unforeseen circumstances. Soon, I'm at the university.

I gaze up at the building. There's nothing special about it at all—it looks like the many other buildings in this neighborhood in Rome—bland, rather plain facades. But this building brought me thousands of miles away from the only life I've known.

Okay, this building and some peer pressure from my friends and gentle encouragement from my kids.

The degree at the end of my one-year MBA program is the carrot, and my ex is the stick.

He can take that stick and shove it up his—

I take a deep breath, thinking about how Sara would tell me to focus my thoughts away from Bruce and toward my successes. She's a yoga instructor and practices mindfulness, and she would tell me that my negative thoughts are hurting me more than they hurt my ex-husband, so I should do my best to encourage my mind back to my school and my success.

I'd always wanted to get my MBA. Bruce and I had talked about it a lot, but it always got pushed to "someday." Well someday is *now*, and I'm going to show Bruce, myself, and my kids that I am a smart, independent woman, and that even after kids and a divorce I can start fresh and be whoever I want to be.

I use that thought to carry me forward. My messenger bag weighs heavily on my shoulders as I take the steps up into the building. A few people are filtering in, too, but not many: men and women, a variety of languages and ethnicities.

What they do have in common is that they are all younger than me.

Like, by a lot.

Like, my kids are closer in age to these people than I am.

My gray hair doesn't help. I'm wearing it down today, and it brushes against my bare arms while I glance down at the paper with my schedule on it. The first week here is an orientation, and the first day is an introduction to the school, the curriculum, and the staff. My schedule says "auditorium," and the people filtering in are all moving in the same direction, so I join the stream and hope I'm going the right way.

I've read the school's brochures and statistics. Most people are late-twenties, early-thirties, with at least five years of related work under their belt. I have fifteen years' experience running the small business that Bruce and I started together, Second Chances, but I'm not sure what that qualifies me for.

It was enough to get into the program, and that's what matters, I suppose.

The auditorium hums, but it's not crowded. I pick a spot in the middle row, a few seats between me and anyone else. No one has their laptops out, but a few people have tablets or notepads, so I leave my computer in my bag and pull out a spiral notebook. I bought a stash of them, and they bring me back to my school days. If only I could have tracked down a Lisa Frank notebook or at least some stickers.

I do, however, need a pen. Rooting around in my bag, I cannot find any writing utensils. I could have sworn I packed one. I remember putting a pen on the little coffee table in my apartment.

This bag isn't that old. How are there already crumbs and grit in the corners of the pockets? And is that…

I pull out a smooth and thin square object. Yup, that's a condom. No doubt Jade's handy work.

Glancing up, I see that the guy three seats down has noticed me and my condom. My cheeks heat. I'm going to kill Jade.

Returning it to the pocket whence it came, I smile through my excruciating blush.

"I was looking for a pen. Do you have any? Pens, I mean, not…" I gesture vaguely. Or at least, I hope it's a vague gesture. "Prophylactics."

"I have a pen," he says without meeting my eye. But he reaches into his bag, a leather satchel, and retrieves a blue pen.

"Thank you," I say, and pull out my phone, diverting my attention to anywhere but the young kid I just used the word *prophylactics* in front of.

I open our group chat.

EMMA

Great. The only words I've said to another student so far have been while holding a condom.

JADE

See? I knew you would need it. Aren't you glad I shoved it in there?

(That's what she said)

EMMA

I'm not having sex with him!

JADE

Why not?

Okay, just kidding. I only snuck it in because I want you to be safe and have some fun.

EMMA

You are lucky I love you so much.

JADE

I love you too.

Go learn stuff! Be awesome!

TESSA

Have a great first day at school Emma!

SARA

We love you!

JADE

Go kick some MBA ass!

That's followed by a bunch of school-themed GIFs, from Nemo to cute kids to Grease, which ends in a naughty school-girl one sent from Jade. I roll my eyes.

EMMA

You had to make it smutty, didn't you?

JADE

Don't kink shame! I like the way my legs look in pleated skirts.

And the spankings. You can't have a naughty schoolgirl fantasy without the spankings.

TESSA

Your legs look great in everything, sweetie.

JADE

Challenge accepted.

I shake my head at Jade's antics. Tessa is right; Jade looks great in everything. She's petite, the complete opposite of my wider shoulders and hips and height. But if there's one thing my friends have taught me in the months since the divorce, it is that clothes do make you feel sexier.

The dress that I wore last weekend, for example, when I went home with Santo. I definitely felt sexy in it.

Then the chat with my friends devolves into Jade sending increasingly ridiculous outfit ideas. The last one I see before I exit the chat is a guy with a black bowl cut and what looks like a bright green *inflatable* crop top.

My kids have also sent messages. It's a group chat with the four of us: my oldest, Gabby; my middle child, Hattie; and my youngest, Parker.

It's 8:30 a.m. here, which means it's 11:30 p.m. back in LA, where Parker is in school. I thought Austin was progressive, but they wanted to go even further. Parker is living their best life right now, studying journalism, surfing in the mornings, and hanging out in gay bars at all hours of the night.

Which means I am not surprised to see a message from them that came in fifteen minutes ago.

PARKER

Happy first day of school mom

EMMA

Thank you. Now go to bed! Don't you have class tomorrow?

PARKER

Not until 10 and im working on an assignment. Youll understand when youre older

EMMA

When I'm older?

PARKER

Technically true. I bet two weeks from now youll be staying up late to work on school stuff. Haha

EMMA

I'm rolling my eyes. Go to bed and eat your vegetables.

They send a kiss emoji back just as a throat at the front of the room clears. A white man who looks to be in his forties stands at the podium. Behind him on stage are a few rows of seats, all of which are filled with, I presume, staff. The room quiets, and anticipation bubbles in my chest. This is it. I'm finally starting my MBA.

The man introduces himself as the director, welcomes us, the students, and gives us an overview of the university's history. The website says everything is taught in English, but I'm still relieved that this is, in fact, in English.

I look around the room in front of me. The students are mostly white and young, but a good percentage of them are Asian. Everyone is dressed so well, too. I look down at my own clothes. I'm wearing slacks and a button-up blouse, but I already feel frumpy in America. Here, everyone is fashionable and chic whereas I wear mom-jeans.

It's okay, I am a mom. Thrice.

We've moved on to professor introductions. As the director announces their names, they stand and wave.

I might get mistaken for a professor. They're closer to my age. Hell, I might be older than some of them.

While I recognize the courses and specialties of the professors being introduced, it's a lot of names to remember, so I don't pay a lot of attention until one name stands out.

"—Santo Offredi—"

I freeze, eyes wide as I watch Santo, the hunky Italian silver fox who tried to give me my first non-solo orgasm in years, stand up from his seat and wave to the crowd.

Oh, my god.

Please don't let him be teaching my classes, please don't let him be teaching my classes...

"Mr. Offredi will teach many of your business fundamentals courses, especially financial basics. He has an extensive background with startups and technology companies, and was named our Educator of the Year last year."

I sink into my chair. Not that Santo—oh crap, Professor Offredi—has noticed me. The first six months of the program are divided into six-week terms, where we have four classes a day. I cannot believe my bad luck. Of all the hot, nice, sexy men in my age range in Rome who happened to be in the right bar on the right night and who met the approval of my friends and who was actually interested in me, I had to pick the one who is my professor?

7

Santo

I AM NOT SURE IF IT'S BEING ON STAGE IN FRONT OF THE ENTIRE student body or if there's something else going on, but the skin on the back of my neck prickles like someone is staring at me. I tune out the speaker for a few minutes, casting my gaze through the students in the seats, but no one really meets my eye. They're too busy paying attention, as they should be.

I direct my gaze back to Director Greco, but the feeling intensifies. When I glance back out at the audience, a flash of movement catches my eye.

Someone is slouching, sitting perfectly behind another student, so I can't see them, but I can see their bag on the seat next to them.

I shift to the left, and I glimpse long, loose hair before it shifts out of my sight.

Gray hair.

My heart unnecessarily speeds up, as if there aren't millions of people in Italy with gray hair, people who aren't Americans who are probably back home and back to their regular jobs.

People who are avoiding me.

I quickly lean over to my far right and bump into Vincente.

"What are you doing?" he hisses at me with an elbow nudge.

"Nothing, sorry," I mutter.

I saw a face. *Her* face.

That can't be right.

Several excruciating minutes later and multiple admonishments from Vincente, I still haven't seen her face again. We've been playing a game of hide-and-seek, and I'm pretty sure the person she's hiding behind is getting concerned by the way I'm staring at them. They have slunk down in their seat. At first, she slunk down, too, but now she's holding a spiral notebook up in front of her face as if she's reading.

I grind my teeth together.

I thought—no, assumed—that she was visiting on holiday. When I picked her up at the bar, I was thinking I'd be a one-night-stand, some fond memory she'd have of her trip to Rome, a story she could brag about to her girlfriends later. *"Remember that Italian man I slept with in Rome?"* she'd say.

Of course, after she ran out, the story changed.

"Remember that Italian man who took me to his place and did something so unspeakable I had to run out in panic?"

And after today it's, *"Remember that Italian man who tried to make me come, and now I'm going to see him around campus all the time?"*

Oh god. It's my turn to sink down in my chair. What have I done?

"…have a fantastic first week getting to know the university and your fellow students. Thank you for your attention, and I'll be seeing you this afternoon," Director Greco finishes.

I dart to my feet, but I'm too slow. Emma—if that is Emma —is ducking down and hiding behind her colleagues as they shuffle out the door toward the break-out rooms where they will meet to begin their tours.

I'm not leading a tour, but Vincente is. Assigned to an activity room, I meet with students, shake hands, explain the facilities, and welcome them to the university.

All morning, I keep an eye out for Emma, but I don't see her. You would think that as tall as she is, as remarkable as her gray hair is, I'd easily find her, but in a crowd of a hundred students filtering in and out, it's hard to spot her.

Especially if she's avoiding me.

Vincente and I grab a quick lunch, then have a faculty meeting, followed by a few one-on-one meetings with students I'll be advising.

When I catch a break, there's a knock on the cracked open door, and Director Greco steps in.

I stand. It's been a few weeks since he joined, just in time for the start of the full-time program, and we've seen a lot of each other, but not one-on-one yet.

We shake hands and I offer him the seat across the desk and settle back into my own once he sits.

The new director doesn't waste time. "I was impressed to see your name on the list of faculty here," he says, folding his hands in his lap. "I was a big admirer of your father's."

"Thank you," I say because people don't like it when I say anything else. They don't want to know that, in addition to being one of the richest men in Italy, my father was a tough man. Even beyond his aspersions for my career: my father was an adulterer.

"His acquisition of MDK Shipping in the seventies really gave Italy a foothold in the US, and his early adoption of sports team sponsorships was brilliant foresight."

"Yes, it was." Sure, that's when my father was brilliant. Not when I suggested investing in cars in the eighties or mobile technologies in the nineties.

Do I sound bitter? I shouldn't be. I made those investments myself and they did very well.

"It makes sense that his son would be a leadership expert. You learned it at home." He smiles and I hold in a sigh. "Do you still do any work for Offredi?"

"I never did any work there," I correct. "And as you know, it's owned by a private equity firm now, and I have never had anything to do with them."

"I see." He nods, more serious now. "And how was your first day of the FTMBA program?"

Fine, fine. The woman I tasted last weekend and spent the entire week fantasizing about is in the program. How does that sound, director?

I come up with some bland response, and after a few more minutes of small talk, Director Greco leaves me alone to get back to my work, but the conversation about my father lingers. I've been a professor here for long enough that most people don't bring it up, despite the business being a household name—as much as an importation company can be, anyway. The only people who really know about my father's more sordid behavior are my ex-wives and Vincente.

And my father's mistress and her daughter.

When I was five, I came home to my mother drunk and crying in my father's home office. My father had had an affair with his very young secretary, who approached my mother when she got pregnant.

Years later, I was able to piece together more and more of that time in my life. My father gave his mistress money to disappear. He never spoke one word about my half-sister or the affair, and my mother's mental health deteriorated. By the time I found out about my sister, my father and I were fighting more and more, and I didn't have the resources to do anything about it.

It was only after my father died and inexplicably left me all his money—but not the business—that I had the means to find her. I hired a private investigator. We stayed in touch long enough for me to give her half the inheritance, and then she said she wanted nothing to do with me. She was happily married with several children and wasn't thrilled to have a reminder of her absent father.

She wasn't thrilled to inherit either, but all that money doesn't make up for a family and a stable childhood.

These thoughts linger until, finally, it's the end of the day, and I can lock up my office and head home. First days of the program are hard. In a work environment, like in the last startup that hired me as CFO, everyone else knows everyone else, and it's you who's new. There's a relative sense of order, of everyday activities that, if you are lucky, you don't disrupt too much.

Not so here. There's a different excitement. Students who don't know each other creating energy in a new way.

It's exhausting.

I exit the building and turn toward home. It's mid-afternoon, as most days end around four o'clock for us, and while the students finished about half an hour ago some of them still linger in a nearby caffè, chattering in a mix of English and Asian languages.

An espresso is tempting, but before I can stop for one, I catch a flash of gray and soft blue across the street.

There, on the opposite sidewalk, is Emma.

Or at least, someone who I'm pretty confident is Emma.

Before I even know what I'm doing, I shout her name. "Emma!"

She turns, but a bus passes, one of the bright red city buses that slams on its brakes and honks at another car, completely blocking my view of her. I walk left, trying to see around it, but by the time I make it, she's made a turn and is walking away from me.

I impatiently wait at the intersection, throwing up my hand and an expletive when I almost get run over by a Fiat.

She's too far to shout again, and I don't even know what I'm going to say when I catch up to her, but it feels imperative that I do. She's walking toward my apartment anyway, I reason.

When I get close enough to shout again, I do, but this time, she doesn't turn around. We're two blocks from my apartment now, and I'm out of breath. Sure, I get plenty of exercise playing football, but usually, I'm not laden down with a bag and a sports coat.

God, I hope I don't have a heart attack chasing after a woman. How ironic.

"Professor!" someone else calls.

It's Eva walking her dog, the brown, chubby French bulldog, toward me. Her smile is wide, and she catches my arm. "How is the new term? Did you have a good start?"

Emma turns the corner up ahead. Assuming she's going home, she'll walk right past my apartment to get to and from university every day.

"Excuse me," I say to Eva, and dart around her.

I ignore the call of my name behind me, and as I turn the corner, I see Emma darting into my apartment building. What?

I run and catch the first vestibule door right before it closes and scramble with my card to catch the second one. "Emma!"

She spins around with a flash of bright red and terror on her face. In the time it takes to process the can of spray—bright red with a black silhouette of a large angry dog barking on it—Emma's no longer scared but surprised.

"Santo? I mean—Professor."

I hold my hands up, palms facing her.

"Oh, my god. I thought you were someone else."

"Who did you think it would be?" She was scared... of who?

"There was this guy this morning. I thought..." She blinks and shakes her head, her hand trembling.

I lean in, anger coursing through me. My voice comes out rough. "Is someone bo—"

The door behind me slams open, and a dog barks aggressively. Reflexively, Emma's eyes widen and her hands tighten. Almost in slow motion, while I'm staring right at it, the mist of pepper spray hits my face.

8

Emma

"Ah!" Santo screams.

"Che cosa sta succedendo qui?" Eva shouts.

Oliver, as usual, barks his head off.

"Oh my god, oh my god. Santo, I am so sorry," I cry.

He's bent over, hands on his eyes, hissing between his teeth.

"What were you thinking?" he shouts.

"You followed me!" I shout back.

"I live here!"

"You live here?"

"Yes. Che due coglioni! Porca miseria!" A lot of other words follow, all of which are, I'm pretty sure, curse words. Eva is shushing her dog.

"It's fine," I tell her. "We're fine, everything's fine."

She eyes me but drags her yappy dog up the stairs.

Despite spending most of the day thinking about Santo while simultaneously trying to avoid him, when I heard my name being called on the street, my mind had immediately gone to the man this morning at the coffee shop instead of Santo.

Santo stands quickly and turns away from me. He's shaking his hands off as if they're wet from a public bathroom that doesn't have paper towels, and his eyes, which are squinting, and the surrounding area are all red too. And wet. Again, like he splashed his face in a public bathroom without checking the paper towels first.

I stand in the corner like a child in trouble. My nerves were so on edge today, between the coffee shop guy and then worrying all day that I would run into Santo, *plus* the first day of school nerves. I nearly left entirely, but Sara, Tessa, and Jade calmed me down. I was in such a panic we actually video chatted in the middle of the day while I hid in an empty computer lab. Of course, though, Jade's solution when she found out he was one of my professors was to ask him for a do-over.

A DO-OVER!

This man knows what I taste like. This was already a DEFCON-1 emergency *before* I pepper-sprayed him. There is no asking for do-overs, even if Santo—damn it, Professor What's-his-name—is just as gorgeous in daylight as I remembered.

He pinches the bridge of his nose, closing his eyes and taking deep breaths.

"I can take you up to my apartment," I offer. "I think I have milk. We can wash your face wi—"

"I'm going to my apartment," he cuts me off. "Just..."

There doesn't seem to be an end to that sentence. After a moment, he drops his hand and squints at the staircase before shuffling forward and hitting the first step with the toe of his loafer. He grips the handrail. He can't see, and this is all my fault.

"Okay, San—Professor. Here." I grab his bicep with both

hands and step closer to him. "I'll get you to your apartment."

His grip on the rail tightens, but he doesn't argue. I help him up the stairs, all the while, his muscles are flexing under my hand. I try to ignore it, but it's hard. Maybe Jade has been right all along, and I really do need to have sex with someone because this situation should not be sexy at all.

"Which apartment is yours?" I ask. He's on the same floor as mine, on the other side of Eva and Oliver, who huffs at the base of the door as we walk past. Santo fumbles his keys, and I help him find the right one and enter his apartment.

His place, unlike mine, is a newly renovated one. It's more modern, with bright blue accent walls and a white kitchen, which I lead Santo to.

I leave him with two hands on the counter and open his fridge, hoping to find some milk, but there's none. That's what they say to drink when you eat something too hot, at least back in Austin, so maybe it would help to flush out someone's eyes? I've dealt with the consequences of unintended jalapeno—or worse—consumption one too many times, which is what happens when you have kids, and your favorite restaurant is a Tex-Mex joint in South Congress.

I hear a faucet turn on, and when I look back at Santo, he's at the sink scooping handfuls of water onto his face. He gasps between each splash. I lean against the counter, curling around my arms, cradling my stomach, and wait. Part of me thinks I should leave, but what if he has an allergic reaction or if the burning doesn't go away? He'd need help.

After a while, Santo leans back, turning off the sink. He holds out his hands and looks down at himself—the crisp, gray jacket he was wearing over a white button-down is soaked. Reaching for a towel first, he dries his hands and face. He still looks quite red and irritated, but it seems he can see now.

"Santo, I'm—"

He holds up a hand, cutting me off. Oookaayyyy, not ready to talk yet. Slowly, he peels the jacket off and then his shirt, leaving a white sleeveless tank top behind. We would call it a wife-beater back home, which is a gross name for something that…well, I guess back home it's pretty gross, period. But here, in the soft light of Santo's kitchen, it's a bit more Marlon Brando in *A Streetcar Named Desire* with sweat and muscles and…

I snap my gaze up to Santo's just before his eyes meet mine. And then they flick to behind me, and they widen.

"Merda! Zola!"

"What?" I ask as he lurches to the door.

"My cat!"

"Your cat? You have a cat?"

He ignores me, whipping around. "A black cat. Check the hallway."

Holy hell in a handbasket, this can't get any worse.

Santo's crouching on his knees checking under the couch so I step into the hallway in time to see a flash of black by the stairs.

I follow it up, and when the hallway comes into view, it is, in fact, a cat. It sits at the far end under the small window, licking its paw.

We had a cat when I was growing up, but Bruce was a dog person, and I was pretty ambivalent about it. We had a golden retriever that died when the kids were in high school —Buffy was her name—but I haven't been around pets since then.

"Hey, gorgeous," I say.

The cat ignores me, but it's in a way that obviously, pointedly says *I'm ignoring you.*

"What did your daddy say your name was?" I croon, feeling ridiculous, but also, if I let this cat slip by me after the day I've had, after the day Santo has had…well, he just might fail me. Or kick me out. Or whatever is in his power to do.

I tiptoe forward while the cat continues to ignore me. "Miss Zola, I think that was your name, right?"

I get a few feet from her and crouch down. She stops licking and blinks at me, squinty-eyed, which makes me think of Santo and his pepper-sprayed gaze.

Like she's trying to guilt me.

That's not funny.

Okay, enough anthropomorphizing, Emma. The cat *does not* understand what you did or why her daddy is upset.

Extending my hand, I hold the back of it out for Miss Zola to sniff. She stares at me like, *what the fuck am I supposed to do with that, lady?*

I'm sure if she understood what I'd done to her dad, she'd be miffed at me.

"Zola? Emma?" Santo calls from downstairs.

"Up here," I answer.

I hear the thud-thud-thud of Santo, who must be taking the stairs two at a time, and soon he's striding down the hallway to retrieve his wayward cat. She stares up at him, tail flicking and curling at her feet.

He says something to her in Italian. "Tu, diavolo subdolo. Non vuoi perderti nel tuo nuovo quartiere, vero?"

The view of Santo, his hands on his hips, white shirt, gray slacks, frowning down at his cat, who continues the conversation with a little *meroooww,* makes me melt. As if I didn't find Santo attractive enough, now he has to talk to his cat, all adorable-like.

He bends down at the same time Miss Zola stands on her hind legs and reaches up to him, and I actually coo out loud while he grabs her under the arms like a toddler and lifts her up. Her whole body goes long and soft, like some weird cross between a slinky and a set of novelty handcuffs.

Santo puts both stretched out paws over one shoulder and moves a hand under her butt, supporting her. Miss Zola curls up, and they both look at me.

Miss Zola looks smug as hell.

Santo looks exhausted.

"Sorry. For the pepper spray and the door."

"Yes. Okay." He takes a big breath, and his cat headbutts his cheek. He says something else to her in pretty Italian, but it's too low for me to even guess what it is.

"So," he says to me, his accent thicker than ever. "We are neighbors."

"Yes."

"And I'm your professor."

"Yes."

"Merda."

My sentiments exactly.

9

Santo

IT TAKES A FEW HOURS FOR MY EYES TO FEEL NORMAL AGAIN. Zola is back in my apartment, Emma is back in her apartment, and I've had some time to calm down.

It's much easier to think with a clear head, though after a long day and being pepper-sprayed, my eyes are tired enough to give me a headache. I'm on the couch, wearing my reading glasses and trying to read a recently published paper on environmentalism in the battery industry.

It's also much easier to relax when I've got a four-kilo purring ball of fluff sitting on my chest. Zola in her favorite position, ass in my lap and face-planted between my pecs. Lord knows how she breathes.

Emma had been scared. It hadn't really been my intention to chase her down. I honestly don't know what I'd been thinking. But looking back at it now, I can see that I made her uncomfortable.

And in her new home, no less.

With a sigh, I move Zola off my chest. She hisses at me, but she's all smoke and no roast. She'll get over it.

A few moments later—after I make sure Zola remains inside and the door closes properly—I'm knocking at Emma's apartment. There's a smell in the air—sweet and warm. I think someone is baking.

Emma opens the door. She's changed into loose cotton pants and a T-shirt. It's a tight T-shirt that says "Save the Ta-Tas" on it with big pink handprints over her breasts. I tear my eyes away and back up to her face. Her cheeks are rosy, and the smell of sugar and spices gets stronger.

"Hi," she says, a little guarded.

Right. Out with it. "I wanted to apologize."

Her eyes widen.

"I didn't mean to scare you."

Emma's body relaxes against the door. "You actually didn't—" she starts, but a timer going off in her apartment interrupts her. "Oh, hang on, that's the cookies. Why don't you come in?"

She walks away, leaving the door open, and I step into the apartment. Like mine, the ceiling is bare wood rafters, but that's where the similarities end. This is one of the unrenovated apartments offered at a reduced rate to students. The kitchen is along the right wall and small—almost more kitchenette than full kitchen—and there's a loveseat and low table facing away from me and toward the outside wall, with a tall window over a dining table.

On the armrest of the loveseat is an open laptop, and a chilled glass of wine sits opposite it on the coffee table, freshly poured and condensing.

Noises draw my attention back to Emma, who is pulling a cooking sheet out of the efficiency oven using kitchen towels to protect her hands.

"It smells good," I offer as she places the hot pan on the stovetop.

"Well, that's good," she says, putting the towel aside. "I made them for you. Unless you have a nut allergy?"

"No allergies," I say, leaning in to look at the cookies. Chocolate chip, it looks like. "What nuts are in there?"

"It's got almond butter in it. They're vegan cookies, so the almond replaces the butter and eggs. I'm not vegan," she hastens to add, "but one of my best friends is. And she introduced these "best ever vegan chocolate chip cookies" to us, and well, they are really damn good."

"Was this the friend you were with?"

Emma, who's already flushed from the heat of cooking in a small space, blushes even further at the non-mention of *that night*. "Yes, that's Sara."

"I had thought that you ladies were on vacation," I admit.

"We were. I mean, they were. They all live in Europe too, so we came together for a weekend here to, I guess, drop me off at school."

"This in unbelievable," I say. "I've been single for years, and have brought home plenty of women, but I have never brought home a student." I run my hands through my hair and curse again.

Emma waves at the loveseat. "Sit," she says. "These need to cool."

Perching on the arm of the loveseat, I watch her carefully maneuver the parchment paper from the baking sheet to the counter and then rip off a section of fresh paper to line it again. "I owe you an apology, too. It wasn't your fault that I was on edge."

What? Oh right. Just before she pepper-sprayed me, she mentioned a guy. "Who is bothering you, Emma?"

Emma reaches into a bowl and pulls out a glob of dough. She thinks carefully before answering, paying a lot of attention to the ball of dough and not to me.

"There was this man this morning who was following me," she says at last, placing the dough on the parchment paper.

My hands tighten into fists. "Where? When?"

"Well, so far, it was just this one run in with him this morning. I shouldn't have told him my name, and it had me jumpy. So, when you called my name, but I didn't know who it was, I freaked out a little." She gives a tight laugh. "This happens in Italy, I know that. I just wasn't expecting it to be so personal."

I straighten. "Who is it?"

She shrugs, still working on rolling cookie dough. "Just some guy."

"What did he look like?"

"Tall, dark hair, olive skin. He was Italian—"

"We're all Italian!"

Emma throws up her hands. "I don't know! I'm not a police sketch artist." She closes her eyes, and I force my hand to unclench. She shakes her head. "No, I don't remember. I would recognize him if I saw him but can't...I don't know how to describe his face."

My gut twists. It was bad when I thought I had been the one responsible for scaring her. I knew my own intentions, but some idiot harassing her is an actual problem. Emma shouldn't be wary in her own home, her own neighborhood, and the Via dei Banchi Nuovi has gotten a poor start. "If you see him hanging around, you tell me, okay?"

At that, Emma looks up, giving me a long stare before she answers. "Okay, I will."

With a few swift movements, the new cookies are in the oven, and Emma has balled up another piece of dough. She takes the two steps from the oven to offer it to me. "Cookie dough?"

I take the ball and bite in while Emma fixes herself one. The dough is gritty from the sugar and greasy, but I hardly taste the almond butter over the sweetness. The chocolate chips crunch under my teeth, and I have to admit, the dough itself is very good.

"How are your eyes?" Emma asks.

"Much better, thank you."

She's taken a small bite of her dough ball, and she plays with the remainder while she chews. Her hands are greasy too. "I've never pepper-sprayed anyone before. It was a learning experience, though I'm sorry it happened."

I pop the rest of the dough into my mouth and lick my fingertips before rubbing my hands together. Seeing Emma was such a surprise today, but as I stand here with her, eating raw cookie dough, it occurs to me that this is an opportunity to ask some questions and get answers I thought I would have to go without. "Why did you leave that night?"

She groans and moves to the sink to wash her hands. "Damn it. I'm sorry about that, too." She dries her hands on a flour sack towel before facing me again, folding her arms across her chest and leaning back against the counter. "I left because I was too in my head. No one has done that to me in a very long time, and I was worrying about too many things, and it was easier just to go."

Fuck. "I'm so sorry. I didn't mean to make you uncomfortable. You had seemed into it—"

"I was, I was. Or at least, into the idea of it. I mean, I was very turned on." The tips of her ears are pink now too. "But when it comes down to it, I just don't think I'm ready yet. I, uh, haven't been with anyone since my husband. Ex-husband," she adds quickly.

I hesitate before asking. "How long has it been?"

"Oh, um, like four years since he's done that."

What!? No one has gone down on this woman in four years? That's a long time to go without, and clearly there are some mental blocks she needs to work through.

Then a thought occurs to me. "When did you get divorced?"

"A little over a year."

So, the divorce is recent. And that means *years* of…

Okay, this is a dangerous train of thought to be having,

and our conversation has veered into inappropriate territory. Emma must think so, too, because she turns back into the kitchen, brusquely pulling out a spatula and some aluminum foil, bundling up cookies for me.

"Do we need to do something at the school to protect your job?" Emma asks, glancing at me while folding the foil.

I scrape my hand over my beard and think. A few years ago we had a professor who quit to be with a student, but otherwise, there is no policy against relationships. Italy is not quite the United States for protecting gender equality.

Plus, we have a new program director, and I'm not sure how he will enforce policies. Even worse, what if he took advantage of her vulnerability? A few years ago, it came out that a former student had filed a sexual harassment claim at her company. Instead of resolving the issue, the HR Manager harassed her himself.

It would be a risk to approach him, especially since nothing further will happen with Emma.

"No," I say. "My job will be fine."

Emma agrees quickly, and hands me the cookie bundle. "Here you go. Thank you for the apology and again, I am so sorry about the pepper spray. And for running out."

I take the dismissal and wish Emma a good night before stepping out of her apartment and closing the door behind me. Back at home, I bite into a still-warm cookie, the melted chips flooding my mouth with dark chocolate. Damn, this really is a good cookie.

I sigh. She's beautiful, she bakes, she's sweet and shy and sexually repressed. I'm going to see her frequently.

And she's absolutely one hundred percent off limits.

10

Emma

The next week flies by, and I barely see Santo. That doesn't mean he isn't in my thoughts—there's always a twinge of disappointment when I shut my apartment door behind me every day without having seen him—but it's a busy week, and that's probably for the best. I already thought Santo was sexy, but when he came by my apartment to apologize wearing glasses it took him to a whole other level. And that is not what I need to be thinking about.

This first week of school was boot camp, a week where we got oriented about our classes, the campus and the structure of the upcoming year.

The second week is a Growth and Technologies week, which sounded a bit like putting the cart before the horse to me, but it ended up being something I could really relate to. It was about pivoting and taking advantage of technologies, and despite being one of the oldest students, I felt like I had a leg up.

My three grown children keep me fairly up to date on what the cool kids are doing. Parker and I had worked together to create the TikTok channel and online store for Second Chances Boutique. I knew about pivoting, at least the mentality of it.

One thing I missed, though, was the daily phone call with my friends over lunch. It wasn't that uncommon for one of us to skip—like if Jade or Tessa had a lunch meeting or something—but making the call between classes was challenging.

I miss my friends deeply, though. I am not sure if it is because I am so obviously American or much older than everyone else, but the students are cliquey so far. Our classes are in English, but most people speak English as a second language. My language app is teaching me basic Italian, but I haven't picked it up in a few days, and while it would help me run my errands, it wouldn't help me make friends in class.

So, when I sit down on Saturday, two weeks into my MBA program, I have a lot to catch my friends up on. But they are way more interested in talking about my neighbor-slash-professor than anything else.

"Is he actually going to be teaching you anything?" Tessa asks.

"Yes," I answer. I've been so busy talking that my sandwich—tomato, mozzarella, and arugula on a baguette, the ingredients of which I bought from a few shops down the road—is getting mushy. "The first term I have him for Business Analytics."

"That's the next five weeks, right?"

"Yeah." I nod. "I don't have the schedule yet for the second term." Screw it. I take a giant bite of my sandwich, the fresh mozzarella über rich and creamy and the tomatoes bright and fresh. Ugnm…so good.

"Are you excited to have him as a professor?" Jade prods with an eyebrow raise. Having lived with her for a month before moving here, I'm not surprised she'd ask. We had a blast in Madrid together, spending late nights out with her coworkers or just the two of us, eating wonderful food and taking in the city. Without that month of watching and admiring Jade, who's fun and carefree and confident, I definitely wouldn't have talked to Santo at the bar.

I chew and swallow, covering my mouth even though it's a video chat, and we've all seen far worse than ungraceful chewing—heck, a couple months ago we walked in on Tessa masturbating. It was embarrassing in the moment, but became a funny story. Fortunately, Tessa is confident enough to laugh it off. I would have died of embarrassment and wouldn't have been able to look anyone in the eye for a while.

"I don't know," I hedge. "He's so good-looking that I think it will be distracting."

"Yeah, but also wish fulfillment." That dreamy voice is Sara's. The other three of us give her a look and a moment of silence. "What? Did no one else have a hot-for-teacher phase?"

"I did," Tessa chimes in. She's in her apartment in Portugal, which came furnished with bland, neutral decor. At least mine is shabby-chic. "One of the math teachers at my high school was fresh out of his degree, so he was young and very hot. Obviously, I never did anything, but I still get a flutter when I think about his tight butt in jeans. He'd erase the chalkboard, and then I'd pretend I'd forgotten to write the equation down, and so he'd have to write it on the board again."

Jade cackles. She's at home in the apartment we shared in Madrid, and as she leans over in laughter, I can see the corkboard behind her with pictures of her all over the world, including photos of the four of us in Paris and Rome.

Next up on our trips together is visiting Sara in Baden-Baden, and that's a perfect segue to change the topic from my hot professor.

The call ends and I close my laptop and jump two feet in the air when I see a black shape in the window. Logically, I know I'm two stories up, but the void is so dark and odd that it takes a minute for my brain to go from portal-to-another-dimension to a-furry-body.

And then said furry body blinks at me.

Oh, it's Zola, sitting on the small ledge of my window again.

"What are you doing here, Miss Zola?"

She *raows* at me, big golden eyes watching as I stand and approach her. My tall windows open to let fresh air in—the apartment doesn't have air conditioning and I understand that in the summer it's uncomfortable. Since Zola knows me, she might come in if I open the window.

Knows me. Ha. I guess if you consider ignoring a proffered hand *knowing* in cat-speak.

Amazingly, I get the window open without Zola hissing and running away from me. How she fits on this ledge, I'm not really sure. The part of her that was pressed up against the window oozes into my apartment.

Zola ignores me.

I put my hands on my hips. "Does your daddy know you come out here?"

She does not answer.

Should I try to pick her up and take her back home? What if she scratches me? Should I put on oven mitts? I don't actually have any oven mitts.

Maybe I should get Santo first.

As if sensing my intentions to tattle on her, Zola's head swivels toward me, and she blinks those big, yellow eyes of hers.

"Well, what did you expect?" I ask her. "I'm on Santo's side on this. Big cities are dangerous for cats."

She blinks again.

I put my hands together and rub them. "Here goes nothing," I mutter. I reach out a hand and touch her head, stroking the very top. Her ear twitches.

I don't know why I'm so scared of this cat. She does look at me with disdain at worst, aloofness at best. "Good girl, Zola."

I add a second hand and get them around what I think is her shoulders, between her head and the giant poof ball of her body. I do a sort of scoop-and-lift motion, and the next thing I know, I have a cat in my hands. Zola doesn't react at all, her front legs straight out in the air and her lower ones dangling, just like the way I saw Santo pick her up the other week.

"Well, that was rather anticlimactic," I tell her. "You're making me feel pretty silly for talking to a cat so much." I maneuver my hands and—much less gracefully than Santo did—get her curled up in my arms and against my chest.

Out the doorway and down the hall I go. When Santo answers the door and sees me with his cat, he blinks.

I blink too. Santo is wearing a soccer uniform, tall socks, and short shorts putting his knees on display, and the bright red against his olive skin is lovely.

"I carried your cat," I say and then flush. Who am I, Baby Houseman? This isn't the Catskills, and Santo is no Johnny Castle.

Err, well. He does kind of look like Patrick Swayze. Damn it, now I'm thinking about Santo lifting me up in a dance lift, which is laughable because I am no Jennifer Grey, and it's more likely that *I* could lift *him* up.

"Thank god," Santo says, breaking my summer camp fantasies. "I've been looking for her all over. I am sorry, she never used to escape at our old place."

"It's fine," I say as Santo lifts his cat from my arms. She hisses at him, which makes me jump back, though Santo doesn't twitch.

He rolls his eyes. "Sometimes I think I am her least favorite person in the world. Where was she?"

"On my window ledge."

"Hm. Troublemaker," he says. He turns and does a gentle little tossing move, and Zola ends up on her feet on the floor, where she shakes herself, annoyed with the whole situation. "Thank you, again. I've been looking all over for her, and now I will be late."

"To work?" I joke. It's a bad joke, and Santo looks down at himself.

"No, to play football."

Okay, time to get back to my place before I make even more of an idiot of myself. "Well, um…good luck!" I turn and power walk back to my door. Behind me, I hear Santo following, locking his door, and jogging, passing my door just as I close it, giving me one last glimpse at a different side of the man.

I sag against my door. Is this what it's going to be like all year long? If I'm not thinking about how he went down on me, I'll be having weird little fantasies in my head.

Maybe I should move.

11

Santo

THE FIRST MORNING OF THE FIRST TERM GOES AS EXPECTED—A flurry of unfamiliar faces, like the past two weeks, but this time, there's a comfort in knowing that we'll be seeing these same people every day for the next five weeks.

The students are full of questions, and by the lunch break, I'm exhausted. I'm locking my office door when someone calls my name. Down the hall, Vincente approaches.

"Good morning?" he asks.

"Fine," I say with a shrug, and we walk down the hall together. "Want to grab lunch?" I offer.

"Yes. We need to talk."

That doesn't sound ominous at all.

There's a bar down the street from the university that we frequent. It's a former cellar, popular with tourists and partiers later in the evening, but today it's still early, so we have our pick of tables. We order wine and sit down under the arched brick ceiling.

Vincente gets right to the point. "You'll never guess who's in my Managerial Economics lecture."

I school my face blank and sip my wine, a robust house red.

Vincente's eyebrows raise. "You already know," he accuses.

Damn it. I must be losing my touch. I used to negotiate employee contracts and mergers without so much as a flinch, but somehow, I've given myself away to Vincente?

My father would be so disappointed.

"You're using that same face as when I told you the police arrested my son." He leans in, resting his forearms on the table next to his forgotten glass of wine. "So, you know the woman you took home from the bar a couple of weeks ago is in our program?"

"Yes," I admit. "I saw her the first day."

"And you didn't tell me?" Hurt flashes in a quick frown across his face.

"What is there to tell?" I ask, spreading my hands wide. "It was a coincidence, and nothing will come of it."

"Have you talked to her?"

"Yes, briefly." I should tell him she lives in my same building so that even if she wasn't in any of my lectures, I'll be running into her all year long. But I don't. I don't want to make this a bigger deal than it is; I don't want to talk about all the things I've learned about her and scrutinize any future interactions I have with her.

Vincente hesitates before carefully saying, "You know that even though she's older than most of our students, it would still be inappropriate to have a relationship with her?"

"Yes, of course. I said nothing is happening, didn't I?"

Vincente leans back into the booth and sips at his wine. "Something *already happened*, Santo."

He glares at me.

"I cannot undo the past," I point out, which Vincente grudgingly accepts. We talk about other things—the caliber of students and how the new director is doing—and after our glasses are empty and our bellies full, we head back to the university. I'm already bracing myself—my last course of the day has one Emma Chance on the roster.

12

Emma

WHEN I GOT MY SCHEDULE FOR THE FIRST TERM, IT DID NOT surprise me *at all* that I had Santo as a professor for my Business Analytics class.

Earlier today, Professor Vincente Romano and I did a mutual double take when we recognized each other from the bar. I hadn't known that Santo's friend was a professor, too, but perhaps I should have guessed. It was about halfway through his class when it occurred to me that Santo might have told Professor Romano about taking me home and what happened after that. It made me want to crawl under the table. I don't need anyone else at the school knowing about it.

Not that I thought Santo would kiss and tell, but still.

Now, in my fourth session of the day, I enter the room for Santo's—that is, Professor Offredi's—class.

Professor Offredi isn't surprised at all when he sees me, his gaze passing over me with a bland, welcoming look, just like with every other student. The school brags about a one-to-one faculty-and-staff-to-students ratio, so I don't think that I'll *always* have a class with Professor Offredi, but I also suspect that a lot of the "faculty and staff" are people who get more involved in the internships or the development center or even the administration.

I listen to the student introductions. Our schedule isn't like mine when I went to college, where there were classes that met Monday and Thursday, classes that met Tuesday and Friday, and then once-a-week classes on Wednesday. It is a more consistent schedule—every day, four sessions a day from 8:15 a.m. to 4:15 p.m. What's really throwing me off is that lunch isn't until 1:30 p.m., so by the time it comes around, I am starving. I'll have to pack snacks to scarf down in the fifteen minutes between the second and third sessions.

Another thing I've noticed is that we use last names here. I'm *Ms. Chance,* and when Santo—damnit, Professor Offredi—says Ms. Chance, even in his sexy Italian accent...well, I've never wanted to get rid of my married name more.

At the time of the divorce, it hadn't even been a question since my kids had the last name Chance, and, except for Sara, Tessa, and Jade, most people knew me as so-and-so's mom. I mean, I had other friends, but they all had kids who were friends with mine.

When I date someone, maybe it would be nice to go back to my maiden name.

Not that I'm thinking about dating after my fiasco with Sa —Professor Offredi.

Anyway, I would have to think about that more. Some time off in the distant future when I'd fully recovered from the incident.

Based on how uncomfortable I am sitting in Santo's presence right now, it might be a while.

Watching Professor Offredi interact with the class is wildly different from having met him at the bar. While the Santo I met was quietly charming, delivering lines as if it were a foregone conclusion that a man would hit on me, Professor

Offredi is very serious, frowning with intensity as he listens to each student's introduction.

He is *very* handsome. Around the room, quite a few people have their eyes on Professor Offredi instead of their fellow student. Has he ever been involved with a student before? Probably not. Or at least, if anyone knew about it, they'd have fired him, right?

His gaze meets mine, and I hope I don't have a dopey expression on my face.

Oh, look at my professor; he's so dreamy.

I straighten up. The entire class is staring at me. I'm sitting at the end of the row, and I guess the people behind me have finished. Whoops, my turn. I've had two weeks of introductions to nail mine down, so even Professor Offredi's gaze can't make me waiver.

"Hello, I'm Emma Chance. I have a background in small business management and marketing and am from Austin, Texas."

It's short and sweet, less information than most people share, but I've seen in this time that everyone—and I mean *everyone*—is more qualified to be here than I am.

The class moves on, and our professor goes over the curriculum for the next five weeks and explains how the grading structure works. None of it is surprising, and Professor Offredi assigns us reading and videos to watch for homework.

When we're dismissed, I gather my notebook and pack my things up. I'm done for the day, thank goodness, and am looking forward to a glass of wine and a lie-down. Before I can stand up, though, someone stops in front of my table.

I look up at a Black woman with box braids and a bright blue and yellow scarf holding them back. I've seen her around in the all-student sessions and in passing. She grins at me. "I hear a fellow American." She's got a general American accent, so I can't place where she's from, but her smile is broad and she offers me her hand. "Shonda."

"Emma," I say. "Where are you from? Sorry, I must have missed your introduction."

"DC. And you're from Austin?"

I sling my bag over my shoulder as I stand, and we exit the class together. "Yeah. Or at least, that's where I lived for decades. I was born in the panhandle, though."

We chat on our way out, comparing schedules. When we get to the street, Shonda hooks a thumb over her shoulder. "I'm this way."

I hook mine in the other direction. "That way."

"Wanna swap numbers so we can talk about the homework?" she asks.

We do, and I walk away excited to have made a new friend.

13

Emma

THE NEXT FEW WEEKS FLY BY. THE FIRST WEEK OF THE TERM WAS hectic since I needed to stay ahead in my classes so I could take the weekend off to visit Baden-Baden with my friends. It was a nice break–we went hiking and to a nude spa, and they teased me a little about Santo, but Sara got most of the teasing when she told us she'd kissed her roommate.

Back in Rome, I throw all my attention into school. Second Chances Boutique, the furniture-flipping business I ran with Bruce, taught me a lot, but it was all so practical. Now I'm learning the theory.

I learn how to approach strategic partnerships—like when Second Chances partnered with a flea market—and what the hell a supply curve is—our pieces were always one-offs—and, in Santo's class, we dig way deeper into familiar financial statements than I had ever been before.

But the classes are hard, and being in the room with Santo is even harder. Sometimes, his gaze snags on mine, and heat flashes through me. I don't know if he feels it too—he doesn't let it show if he does—but it makes me lose my breath, and if I'm not careful, my mind wanders back to that night.

It's such a distraction and one I really don't need.

Adding to that, Santo is easily the most engaging professor we have. Before getting accepted, I'd read some pros and cons of this program and one con that was mentioned often—not just at this school but at European schools in general—was that teaching styles differed from American schools. Professors would be more aloof, building less of a personal relationship. After reading the bios of the faculty here, I wasn't surprised; they all write papers and books and do consulting and researching. Where would they find the time?

But Santo does. His lectures are popular. There are whispered rumors about how he mentored the guy who's startup just had a record-breaking IPO on the Borsa Italiana or that one of his former students invited him to Stockholm when she accepted a Nobel Prize in Economic Sciences.

My fellow students idolize him.

November first is All Saint's Day, a national holiday in Rome, and because I'm eight and nine hours ahead of my children, I wake up to pics of them in costume, and I worry all day about them. After Zoe's recent brush with drugs—though it was just pot and apparently it wasn't her first time—and my kids being out partying in three different major cities, and dear god, what if something happens to more than one of them? Bruce can only be in so many places at once, and I'm an ocean away.

I don't get a lot of schoolwork done. I don't want to go all mama-bear on my kids since they *are* adults now. Plus, even if I asked them to let me know when they get home, odds are pretty good that they've been drinking and will forget.

So, the next day, in classes, I'm not fully firing on all cylinders when Santo starts on our last module of the term—Sustainability Reporting.

Specifically, I get tripped up on learning about the Triple Bottom Line. When I was working in the business with Bruce, we didn't consciously think about things like sustainability as it relates to our bottom line. Our bottom line was the regular old *single* bottom line—profits. I used QuickBooks to run Profit and Loss statements, which Bruce barely looked at, but I really like the idea of a triple bottom line, considering the environment and the people instead of just profits.

Santo turns to the class after drawing a visual representation of a TBL and asks, "What steps can we take to improve how our business is doing in terms of taking care of our people?"

Hands go up and Santo calls on my classmates, who suggest paternity leave and medical benefits, with a few jokes at the expense of my home country. Analyzing competitive salaries and remote work and wellness benefits.

I think back to my time at Second Chances. We started with just Bruce and me but grew quickly as HGTV shows became popular. We opened up a storefront in Austin about ten years ago and celebrities like Chip and Joanna Gaines made remodeling and refurbishing trendy again. Then social media took off and our business pivoted to online orders.

By the time Bruce asked me for a divorce, we had ten employees working in our shop on furniture pieces, two buyers, and a team for the store, and revenue approaching ten million a year.

What did we do to boost our people?

I raise my hand. Santo's eyes snag on me. My blush is creeping up. It's not like I haven't talked *at all* in class, but having all eyes on me is always intimidating. Austin is metropolitan and full of culture, but in this international, highly educated crowd, I feel like a country bumpkin.

"Em—I mean, Ms. Chance."

Well, okay, now it's definitely a full blush at Santo nearly using my first name.

I clear my throat. "What about holiday parties? And bringing your staff lunch?"

"Excellent," Santo says, and I can't help but smile. A few more people make suggestions and then he asks the same about the Environmental bottom line.

Hands fly up.

Santo chuckles and calls on someone behind me.

"Are you going to run an industry lab again this year?"

Industry labs are toward the end of the program where we do a two-week intensive dive into a specific company. I'd heard about Santo's lab last year, which was by far the most raved about one. It took place at an electric super car company in Romania and in the end, the students' initiative, led by Santo, had resulted in an award-winning zero emissions program.

Santo's industry lab this year is going to be hard to get into based on how excited my classmates are.

"Industry lab programs will be announced at the end of the fundamentals terms." A sly grin crosses Santo's face. "And now back to the question at hand."

The discussion moves on, and the class ends half an hour later, but as I'm gathering my things, Santo calls my name. "Ms. Chance, may I have a minute?"

"Sure," I say, slowing. Shonda waves, her gaze darting between Santo and me.

When it's the two of us left, Santo leans against the podium at the front of the class. "I've had the opportunity to talk one-on-one with many of the students here, as an advisor or giving them additional help with the course work, but you and I haven't talked much about your course work or career."

"Oh, okay. What do you want to know?"

Santo crosses his arms. "Why are you getting your MBA? Why here?"

Oh, I have an answer for this. Jade helped me prepare for

my interviews during the application process. "In Austin, we have a lot of startups and tech companies. But there are also a lot of local, independent businesses, and with this degree, I'll be able to—"

Santo holds up a hand and gives me a crooked smile. "This is not a job interview. I want to know why you, personally, want to get an MBA. What makes this interesting to you, Ms. Chance?"

He wants the real answer, the one that made me leave my kids on another continent and take an enormous risk. I swallow. "My husband started a business when we had young kids—"

"This is the husband who—" He cuts himself off, waving the question away and then gesturing for me to continue.

I flush, knowing exactly what he's thinking about, but I start back up. "It was flipping furniture, buying old pieces and making them new again. He was great at it—at least, he was good at the furniture part. But it was a job he could do on nights and weekends to bring in more money, and he hit a certain point where he said he thought it would make more sense for him to quit his job selling insurance and do the furniture full time. He came to me with the suggestion, and I've always been good at numbers and computers, so with a breast-feeding baby and a toddler on one hip, I taught myself how to make a P&L and showed him he couldn't afford to quit his job—*yet*."

Santo nods, listening closely.

"And it worked. I became the business side while he did the actual work. But it was his name on everything, and even when we started really making money, it was his company." I shrug my shoulders. "It didn't matter how much of the success was because of me. When he told me he wanted a divorce, he was managing a workshop full of custom or luxury pieces, and I was running the storefront, the customers, and the books. He was surprised that I quit. He said he didn't think I had a plan for work."

Santo's eyebrows draw down with concern. I know Bruce could have been nasty about the whole thing, setting the tone for our divorce to be all about money, alimony, and ownership of the business, but he didn't. It wasn't an awful divorce, and I was more sad for our kids than I was for myself.

"It sounds bad, I know, but he had a point. My only reference was Bruce or his employees. I didn't have a formal degree. So, I set out to fix both." My chin tips up reflexively and I brace myself for an inquisition.

Leaning back, Santo uncrosses his arms and grips the edge of the podium with his hands. A small smile plays on his lips, and there's an expression that might be something like pride or admiration. Whatever it is, it makes me soften a tiny bit.

"And why here?"

"Do you remember my friends?" We both freeze at the mention of that night, but Santo gives a small nod. "One of them got a job in Madrid, and then it was like dominos. Another's daughter got accepted into a study abroad program in Germany. One of them worked remotely anyway and had always wanted to live in Europe. That left me. I was looking at local MBA programs, but then one of my kids sent me a link to an international program—not this one, but after looking at a few schools, this one worked out the best."

I raise my arms out from either side of my body. "So here I am. I wanted to prove to myself and everyone else that I could do this independently of Bruce."

Santo stands. "My late father would have liked you."

I wrinkle my brow in confusion, but Santo moves on. He asks more questions about my plans for my concentration and post-degree prospects, and when I leave, I walk away from the university, contemplating fate.

All the decisions—not just mine, but Bruce's, my kids', my friends'—they all ended with me here. And the same goes for

Santo. Our wildly different lives converged, and Santo went from being a total stranger to a huge complication in my life.

I often wish that I'd never met him in that bar, that I'd never pepper sprayed him, and that we didn't live right down the hall from each other. It's complicated and messy.

But also, kind of amazing.

14

Santo

THE FIRST TERM ENDED LAST WEEK AND THE SECOND TERM, A SIX-
week one, started yesterday. I have Emma in one of my
lectures again; this time it's Innovation and Corporate Entrepreneurship.

After our conversation about what brings her to the
program, I had hoped that I could feel more of a mentorship
role toward her, but if she were in my office, I wouldn't trust
myself not to get on my knees and taste her again. I brace
myself with every knock on my door, worried it's going to be
her, and it never is.

I tell myself that it's not disappointment I feel. I don't
form a relationship with most students, just the ones that
seem eager for mentorship and seek me out. If she doesn't
want that sort of a relationship, that's her choice.

I am grateful, though, that Eva is gone most nights and
takes Oliver with her. She's mentioned in passing that she's
staying with her new boyfriend, so while Emma doesn't visit
my office in reality, in my head, she does, and I can satisfy
myself without the dog next door barking at me.

I'm late leaving the university on Tuesday, and it's already pitch black out. The days are getting shorter and more comfortable, but we haven't had any of the autumn rain in over a week and the trees are still green. It's still early in November, and soon the leaves will turn brown and plummet to the ground.

Emma was out of town last weekend with her friends, which I know because I held the door open for her while she left the building with her bags as she rushed out late for the airport. Often, when I pass her door, I have a moment where I wonder what she's doing. Is she studying? Is it for my course?

Today, though, when I reach the top of the stairs, there's a young woman leaning against my apartment door looking down at her phone. "Bell!" I greet my former stepdaughter. "What are you doing here?"

She straightens when I reach her, putting her phone back in her purse, and I bend to buss her cheek. Abelie is almost a head shorter than me, with long dark hair, doe eyes, and a strong nose. "I was in the neighborhood. I messaged you but knew you would be back from work soon."

"Ah, I must not have checked my phone. Sorry, butterfly." I unlock my door and usher her in, flipping the lights on in the dark apartment.

Abelie's mother was my second wife, and though I was only her stepfather for about two and a half years, we stayed close. Her father passed away when she was young, and I married her mother when Abelie was ten. We barely made it through the terrible teenage years, and there were some dicey moments where she tried to use me against my ex-wife, but she quickly discovered that she could not play me that way. Then, she grew to respect it. Now she's at university herself, on the other side of the city, but I still see her about once a month or so, when courses are in session.

"How was your trip to the country?" I ask, putting my messenger bag down on the dining table. There's a soft thump-thump-thump as Zola runs to greet her favorite person—no, not me, who feeds her and cuddles her every night, but my twenty-year-old surrogate daughter.

Bell obligingly turns to the loft stairs and sits on the bottom step. Zola raises her chin, and Bell obediently scratches. "It was lovely. Thank you for letting me use your place."

I have a house in Castel Gandolfo, a small village in The Castelli Romani, that I use during the summer when I don't have lectures and the university's students are off on internships. Bell asked if she could use it last weekend with a friend —I suspect of the romantic variety, but she hasn't volunteered.

We talk a bit about the state of the place—while she was there, I asked her to check on the maintenance and upkeep that one of the local townsmen handles for me—and as we talk, we pour glasses of wine and step out onto my balcony. It faces the street since I have a corner apartment, and I have a small table and two chairs out there with potted plants that Zola likes to destroy.

"What brings you to my part of town, anyway?"

"There are some American foreign exchange students in our architecture program, and they wanted to go see the Vatican, so I came with them to act as a translator to make it easier. We were going to have dinner out, too, but they decided they were too tired." She shrugs. "So, I came to see you."

It's only a half-hour walk to Vatican City from here, a fact my university boasts about. I don't care too much about the Vatican, but I'm glad it brings Bell to see me.

"Can I smoke?" She holds up a pack of cigarettes, and I grimace.

"You didn't smoke inside my house, did you?"

"Of course not."

She kicks her feet up onto the big, glazed pot that houses a fern and lights her cigarette. Zola joins us, and I groan internally when she launches herself up into the big pot and paws at the dirt. She won't use it as a litter box, but she will roll around in it, and I'll have to brush her afterward.

I point at my cat, whose ear flicks. "We have to keep an eye on her. She's been escaping lately."

Bell leans forward and pitches her voice higher. "Such a good kitty. Why are you escaping? Don't like your new house? You still have an entire room to yourself."

I snort and cross my arms. My apartment has one bedroom, but it also has a small loft above the kitchen that has become a dedicated Zola room. She had her own room in the previous apartment, too, the only difference being this one doesn't have a door. A fact that doesn't matter to a cat.

Bell gives Zola one last scratch before she sits back, too.

"You enjoyed the house," I say, changing the subject from my spoiled cat who might rather live with Bell. "Did your friend?"

I'm curious who she deems important enough to take on a romantic weekend. It's nothing nosy.

Bell snorts, though, looking at me out of the side of her eye. "Are you going dad on me?"

I raise my hands. "You don't have to tell me anything, but I want to know what's going on in your life." I've always been in some gray area between father figure and friend. I love her like a daughter, but the dynamic isn't quite the same.

"Well, *she* had a great time." Bell tells me about her new girlfriend, who she's been seeing for three months now. "She's beautiful. Like Mom."

"Like you," I correct.

My stepdaughter waves her hand, the one with the lit cigarette in it, causing the smoke to zigzag in the air. I don't love her smoking, but her mother does it. She quit while we were together, but after we separated, she started up again, and it's my greatest pain leftover from the divorce, which says a lot about my investment in our marriage. "Mom gets all the attention. Men like to pretend they think we are sisters." She rolls her eyes.

The way she says attention draws my mind back to Emma saying she was getting unwanted attention from men around the neighborhood. "Bad attention?" I ask with a frown.

She shrugs. "Sometimes."

My frown deepens, and I hum.

"Why do you ask?"

"My friend—well, my neighbor—she got harassed a couple of months ago. The guy called her and followed her."

Bell frowns. "Calling, yes. Most of my friends have been catcalled. Usually, it's harmless. Not to say that it's okay," she says. "But I have never felt troubled here." She sighs. "There are bad people everywhere."

I don't enjoy thinking about Emma being in danger, so I change the subject back to Bell's girlfriend. But a few minutes later, Bell sits up and looks around. "Where's Zola?"

I curse, looking around. She's not in the pot, though I can tell she was there thanks to the dirt on the balcony floor and the Zola-shaped indent.

Bell waves her cigarette, rising to her feet. "Go look inside. I'll call for her."

Turning, I step inside just as Bell shouts, "Zola!"

I get less than two meters in before a quizzical voice shouts back, "Santo?"

"Yes, do you have his cat?" Bell shouts back, but she's speaking in Italian.

There's a brief pause, and Emma yells back, "I'm sorry I don't speak Italian, but I have Zola!"

"My neighbor," I explain to Bell and then shout back in English, "I'm coming to get her."

Amused, Bell snuffs out her cigarette in the potted plant and follows me into the hallway. Emma's door opens just as we arrive, and Zola is in her arms again.

Lucky cat.

Emma lifts the cat up, and we make the transfer. "I am sorry," I say. Fuck, why am I constantly having to apologize for my little escape artist? "We were out on the balcony, and I lost track of her."

"It's fine. But next time she shows up, I might keep her."

She's joking, I think. Before I can respond, Bell clears her throat, reminding me she's here. "Ah. Bell, this is my neighbor, Emma. Emma, my stepdaughter, Abelie."

The women shake hands and exchange small talk as I stroke Zola's back like a Bond villain. She purrs.

I shift on my feet. I don't know how to act around Emma outside the university without the professor-student facade between us. I wish I could make her smile and flush like I did the night I met her, but I'm frustrated enough as it is; there's no need to torture myself, especially in front of Bell.

When Bell asks what brings Emma to Rome, Emma's gaze finds mine. "Um. I'm a student?" Her voice goes high on the last syllable.

Bell braids her fingers together and sways toward Emma, a mischievous glint in her eyes. "Are you a student at the university?"

"Well, uh, technically, yes." A blush rises on Emma's cheeks.

"Bell," I reprimand.

"What?" She spreads her hands, the same innocent look on her face I saw, frequently, when she was a teen—the one that she uses when she knows exactly what she's doing wrong. "It's a great university. You must be smart to get in. How are you finding it? The first term is over, yes?"

Then I have to listen to Emma discuss her coursework with Bell and that gets them talking about Vincente. I should leave them to it and put Zola back in my apartment, but I look down and tell myself that Zola is comfortable and my unwillingness to leave has nothing to do with hearing about Emma's life outside the university and everything to do with pampering my cat who merely tolerates me.

Finally, the conversation wraps up and we say goodbye. Bell and I troop back to my apartment.

The door shuts behind us, and Bell rounds on me.

"What was that?"

"What was what?"

"You were tongue-tied. That makes no sense. Who was that man out in the hallway?"

"She's my student."

Bell raises an eyebrow. "You also gritted your teeth when I said that Vincente was cute. Might your feelings be more complicated than you know how to handle?" She grins.

"Not exactly," I hedge. "I don't know her very well."

"Well, quit being weird. You should ask her out."

Bell starts to gather her things, and I roll my eyes. "Yes, that will make it less weird. I could get fired."

"Okay, then *befriend* her." She puts her bag over her shoulder and pulls her loose hair out from underneath the strap. "You take things too seriously."

I snort.

Bell kisses my cheek. "Call me next time you are on my side of town."

"Love you," I tell her, even though she annoys me with her insight.

"Love you too."

Bell scratches Zola on the head and calls goodbye, shutting the door behind her.

I sit on the couch before turning and slowly lying down. Zola stands on my chest, all four and a half kilos of her focused on her four paws, which makes it feel like ten kilos hampering my breathing, but then she settles down again.

I stroke her back as she purrs. Will anyone else catch on that I am attracted to my student and that we've already had a near-miss of a fling? The purring rumbles, battling the anxiety in my chest that tells me becoming friends with Emma wouldn't make the situation any better.

15

Emma

I TRY NOT TO BE TOO UPSET ABOUT MISSING OUT ON Thanksgiving. It's a stupid, genocidal, oppressive holiday anyway, and it was fine to not have my kids come home for it, and I didn't want to spend all day cooking a big meal where I would inevitably screw up at least two dishes, but because Parker is a whiz in the kitchen, it would eventually all pull through, and we would sit down to our Thanksgiving day dinner and eat ourselves silly.

I am *living in Rome*. This was way better, obviously, even if I have a full week of classes.

But still.

My kids are even spending it apart, although Hattie is going to be with Bruce and his parents. I wonder if they'd all be together if I had flown home. Bruce and I had discussed holidays in the divorce as if they were custody, and I suppose, since the kids are grown, that's the closest thing to it. Having the kids so far apart now meant that having them all together was harder, so Bruce and I would strive not to force them to split their time between us for the holidays.

Shonda and I decided to host our own Thanksgiving but keep it light. I wasn't sure I could find a sixteen-pound turkey in Rome anyway (or fit one in my oven), so we agreed on roasting a chicken. Shonda offered to make macaroni and cheese and sweet potato pie. Cranberry sauce was the last thing on my list, and two stores didn't have it, but I had found an expat forum that suggested a place on Cola di Rienzo a few blocks from the school. I return home triumphant on Saturday afternoon, and a few minutes later, there is a knock on my door.

I open it, and Santo and Bell are standing outside. Outside of the classroom, I hadn't seen Santo since Zola had come for a visit last week and I'd met Bell.

"Professor Offredi. Hi."

"Ms. Chance," he greets me. "You remember Abelie?"

"Yes, hi." We smile at each other.

Bell folds her arms. "I was wondering if you had plans for Thanksgiving? There is an exchange program at my university, and the American students are hosting an event. They are calling it a potluck?"

"Oh. That's such a nice offer. Um, I have plans with Shonda. You remember her, Professor Offredi? She was in your Business Analytics class with me. But I can ask her if she'd rather do something bigger." I swivel my gaze back to Abelie. "Um, would you be going too? Of course, I mean, would *both* of you be going?"

"I have never been to a Thanksgiving before; have you, Santo?" My neighbor shakes his head. "Yes, we will come. They are roasting quite a few turkeys, and there will be many pies and some stuffing."

I smile. Having someone else do it sounds much better than making stuffing from scratch. "That's all the good stuff. Can I let you know?"

Abelie and I exchange WhatsApp numbers, and I thank them for the invitation. That night, I check with Shonda, and we both agreed that Thanksgiving is typically a the-more-the-merrier situation. Thursday, after class, I scurry home to grab my cranberry sauce and green bean casserole—turkeys were being provided, so I saved the chicken for a later date. I meet Shonda outside my apartment, and a few moments later, Santo pulls up in his car. It's a red sedan, and I notice a cute little shamrock logo right by the door. Is it an Irish car? I don't know anything about cars, but I've never heard of a car made in Ireland.

Santo gets out. Nerves flutter in my stomach. God, he's good-looking. He's still dressed as he was for class today: a fitted jacket and dress slacks.

Shonda jumps in the backseat, so I take the front seat and buckle the seatbelt. "Thank you for driving us," I tell Santo. Abelie's school is on the other side of the city, so she'll meet us there.

"Yeah, and sweet ride," Shonda chimes in from the back. "I've never been in an Alfa Romeo."

That doesn't sound Irish. I bite my tongue, not wanting to sound stupid. It is a nice car, and I smooth the black leather under my thigh with my finger. It's soft.

"You are welcome." He shifts the car into gear and on to the street. It's been a while since I've been in a manual car, and Santo's hand is right there on the gear shaft, just a few inches from my thigh as he zips through traffic. "Your food smells good. What are you bringing?"

I look down at the cold green bean casserole in my lap. I doubt he can smell it at all—I can't. We were told there will be microwaves to reheat food, which is not ideal, but it's better than a cold meal. I catch Shonda's eye in the back seat, and she snickers.

"It's a green bean casserole." I explain the ingredients and Santo repeats them back to me slowly, as if learning a foreign language.

"French...fried...onions?"

"Yes."

Santo looks skeptical but then Shonda leans forward and points toward something ahead of us. She diverts attention from the food and asks Santo about construction traffic in the city. After a few harrowing near-misses and what I can only assume is colorful cursing in Italian by Santo, we arrive at the architecture studio where the Thanksgiving potluck is being held.

I put my green bean casserole on the pre-microwave table, leaving it to the students, who have several microwaves plugged in around the room. They scurry back and forth, heating dishes up. There's a table with drinks—a suspect-looking punch and cases of Dreher, a cheap Italian beer—but a moment later, a stranger grabs my elbow and steers me toward the "adult" drink table, where I pour myself a glass of red.

I find Shonda and Santo again. He's laughing at something she's said, and this might be the most relaxed I've seen Santo since school started. Abelie joins us in a few minutes, kissing my cheek in greeting, and introduces us to some of her friends in the program.

Celebrating Thanksgiving was supposed to be a taste of "normal" life back home. But here, standing with a bunch of students the age of my kids, I find my heart clenching in homesickness. As proud as I am for my acceptance to the MBA program and for coming all the way here out of my comfort zone, I miss my kids. A lot.

There's a cluster of people over in one corner. I can't see what they are doing, but occasionally someone shouts out some numbers.

"One seventy-two-point-three!"

"Two thirty-six-point-eight."

"Abelie," I ask, leaning toward her. "What are they doing?"

"I am not sure; let me ask." She calls across the room in

Italian, and a male student with a clipboard looks up. He answers, and they go back and forth for a moment before Abelie turns back to me, agape. "They are weighing themselves on a scale and having some kind of contest? Who can eat the most?"

My jaw drops. That is my worst nightmare.

Abelie chuckles at my face. "Is this not something all Americans do for Thanksgiving?"

"No. Oh my god, *no.*"

Shonda face-palms. "College kids are so weird."

We all murmur our agreement and watch in fascination.

Someone clears their throat and then a sharp whistle rings out. There's a man standing over by the buffet set up—white, older than me, and wearing jeans and a polo shirt—who is ineffectively clicking his plastic wine glass with a disposable knife. Instead of the *ting-ting-ting* that carries, it's a muffled *bink-bink-bink*, and he continues it for comedic effect once the room is quiet, and a few students chuckle.

His message is brief—dinner is served. There are about thirty people here, but they've got both sides of the buffet going and there is a ton of food. Soon we're perched at a collection of four drafting tables which have had stools pulled up all around to accommodate everyone. Abelie's friends and one of the American professors have joined us, completing our table of eight.

The food is fine, unevenly warmed and heavy, but also very nostalgic. Shonda's macaroni and cheese is probably the favorite and goes quickly.

There's another loud whistle, and the same professor from earlier is standing at one of the tables. "There is an American tradition we'd like to encourage, which is to go around the room and share what we are all thankful for. You don't have to speak, but you are welcome to if you'd like. I'd like to start by saying I'm thankful for the professors and students at our host university who helped us, not only today, but over all the years the exchange program has been running."

He lifts his glass, and we all toast and drink. One by one, we go around the room. Most of the students stand up and speak, and sometimes it's irreverent and followed by laughter —"I'm thankful for two a.m. Kebabs." Sometimes, it's heartwarming and makes the mom in me tear up—"I'm thankful for the technology to FaceTime with my family." And sometimes it's inside jokes that make us three outsiders exchange amused glances.

We get to our table. One of Abelie's friends starts. "I'm grateful for the legal drinking age in Italy," he says with a grin. Everyone groans.

Abelie is next. "I am thankful for my new friends who invited me today."

Then Santo. He stands and rests a hand on Abelie's shoulder. "I am grateful for the best ex-stepdaughter I'll ever have." He looks at Abelie. "You are my family, and always will be."

She smiles, her eyes wet as she leans her cheek on his hand. He kisses the top of her head before sitting down.

My turn. I stand with my glass. "Well, my kids aren't here, so I don't have to suck up to them." There's a chuckle around the room. "I'm thankful for the opportunity to get an education like the one I'm getting now. It's not often that people have to start their lives over in their forties, but having new friends," I lift my glass to Shonda, "and, uh…" I turn to Santo. How to describe Santo? "New neighbors," I finally settle on, "is really helpful."

When I sit, Santo and Shonda clink glasses with me. Neighbor feels so inadequate, but there isn't really a better way to describe him. Santo's gaze catches mine and holds. My heart thumps faster and I can't look away.

Laughter interrupts us, though, and I blink. Santo turns away, sipping his wine. We listen to the rest of the thankfulness, and the lead professor says, "Okay, now that everyone's been thankful, there's pie."

The volume increases while many of the room gets up to help themselves to the dozens of pies on the far table. We stay seated, though.

"You know," Abelie says, turning to Santo with one hand on her hip. "Fifty-seven is not that old. You still have time to marry and divorce and gain more ex-stepdaughters Maybe they'd be older ones, so that you don't have to go through terrible teenage years again." Her tone is light and teasing and Santo laughs.

"Well, I would have to get married first, and I think those days are done for."

I bite the corner of my lip to hide my frown. That's sad. Santo is successful and attractive and the night he took me home, he was certainly charming.

Abelie pouts. "Are you saying I will never have the opportunity to introduce someone as my ex-stepfather's new stepchild?" She catches me following the conversation and winks. I look away, cheeks hot.

Am I going to have stepchildren someday? I love the relationship Santo has with Abelie; loving but still paternalistic. Over the past month, I've thought about sex with new men—well, let's be honest, mostly sex with Santo—but would I ever want to get married again?

16

Emma

THE WEEK AFTER THANKSGIVING IS OUR TENTH WEEK IN THE MBA program, and while I'm enjoying life in Rome, I've made new friends, and I am not getting catcalled nearly as often, academically, it's not going well. I thought that I would have figured this thing out a bit more and would have worked out the kinks of being a full-time student now that we're into my second semester, but alas, this is just how I am as a student.

This week was especially hectic because I wrote down that an assignment for my Organizational Behavior class was due "next Friday," but I had jotted it in the margin of my notes from the week of orientation, so I got my Fridays mixed up. It was due today, not next Friday. Frazzled, I asked for an extension from my professor, and they gave me until Monday, thank god. That means that this weekend I can buckle down and work on it.

I'm leaving my last class of the day, mapping out my path home and how I'm going to swing by a local delicatessen to grab dinner for later when my phone vibrates in my bag.

While taking the steps down to street level from the school's exit, I scramble to find it. I'm glad I did because when I pull it out, it's Hattie's face gazing out at me from the screen. My kids have my schedule, so hopefully she knows I'm just out of class.

"Hey, Hattie!" I answer.

"Mom, where are you?" She sounds out of breath—from excitement, I hope, and not anything bad.

"Just leaving the university and heading home. Where are you?" My middle child is in college in Houston, so I assume she's between classes or having lunch.

"I'm in Rome!" she shouts.

I nearly drop my phone. "What? Where?"

"I'm at a cafe. I'll send you my location. Meet me here?"

"Of course."

The message comes in, directing me to a small cafe in the opposite direction of my apartment, closer toward the Vatican, but that's fine. Hattie's *here*. I have so many questions.

How did she get here? What is she doing? Why is she surprising me?

I have a lot fewer questions after I spot her in the cafe sitting at an outside table. She's not alone—my ex-husband is here, and that provides a lot of answers. I'm guessing this was Bruce's idea, and he paid for the ticket, and Hattie is surprising me because even though I can be a bit of a pushover when it comes to my middle child, I would have put my foot down and said no to Bruce coming here.

I give Hattie a warm hug and revel in that for a moment— it's been almost four months since I've seen her. She seems to feel the same way, and we don't pull apart for so long that Bruce clears his throat.

Reluctantly letting go of her, I turn to Bruce. Maybe it's the residual effect of having been around my friends, a bunch of strong, confident women, over the past few months, but I straighten up to my full height so that I look slightly down at my ex. "Bruce," I say, "what are you doing here?"

"Emma, it's good to see you." He opens his arm for a hug, and I hide an eye roll and quickly return it. We're still trying to find a new normal, especially around the kids, which often means dealing with my feelings of being dropped like a hot potato when our youngest went off to college in private—or at least the privacy of my best friends and some cheap wine.

"So, what *are* you doing here?" I repeat my question.

"Well, Hattie and I were talking about her schedule and since she has Fridays off, we thought we'd take a red-eye and come for a visit. Especially since we didn't get to see you for Thanksgiving."

"Well, a spontaneous visit. How lovely."

"I hope we're not inconveniencing you. I know your classes are in session, but surely you can take some time to tour Rome with us?"

"Of course." Whelp, there goes any free time I had this weekend. But I am excited to spend time with Hattie, and hopefully, I can convince her to do some things solo with her dad.

Bruce pays their bill speaking loudly in English, and if Tessa were here to see this, she would smack Bruce's shoulder and hiss at him to *be cool* while elegantly and apologetically handling the check. I'm pretty sure Jade could do this whole interaction in Italian. One time, she told us she could order a beer in twenty-three different languages.

My friends—well, at least Jade and Tessa—are so much more well-traveled than I am, and two of the four reasons for that are right in front of me. Bruce and I had talked when we were younger about traveling abroad, but those plans never materialized, and that was both our faults. When you run a small business and have three kids, doing something like flying to Paris for an anniversary trip doesn't happen without a shit ton of planning.

I'd shocked Bruce when I'd told him I was going to get my MBA in Rome. Even more shocked than when Parker had come out as non-binary. Almost as shocked as he was when I told him I would not be working for him after he announced that he wanted a divorce.

See where all that falls? Charming, right?

After Bruce pays the bill, I lead the two of them back to my apartment, detouring to show them the unimpressive outside of my university and pausing as we cross the River Tiber at the Ponte Principe Amedeo Savoia Aosta. Gazing down at the water, Hattie points out the running trail to her dad on the bank of the river and they discuss running together in the morning.

"Where are you staying?" I ask them.

"I have a hotel room just down the river. But…" Bruce glances at Hattie, who turns to me with hope in her eyes.

"Could I stay with you, Mom?"

"Of course, but you know I only have one bed, right?"

She shrugs. "That's fine. We can share."

As teenagers, my kids protested so much if they ever had to share a bed with one of us. My how times have changed.

———

LATER THAT NIGHT, AFTER AN EARLY DINNER AND CATCHING THE Trevi fountain all lit up, Hattie and Bruce are too jet lagged for much more, so we split up, Hattie and I returning to my apartment. She falls asleep quickly while I work on my assignment for Organizational Behavior.

Maybe it was years of primarily reading titillating romance novels with my friends or over a decade of experience running a small business, but good god, reading about this stuff is boring as hell.

Maybe it's reading a bunch of stories about old white dudes sucking the life out of labor forces.

Either way, when Hattie came out of my bedroom hours later, rubbing her eyes sleepily and asks what I'm doing, I realize I've gotten off track, and instead of finishing my chapter on the Hawthorne Experiments I was watching a YouTube video on squirrel obstacle courses.

How did I get here?

"I have an assignment due Monday that I forgot about, so I have to work on it this weekend. Sorry, sweetie." Hattie sits next to me on the loveseat and leans onto my shoulder. I kiss her dark, curly hair.

"You forgot about an assignment? That doesn't sound like you."

"Well, apparently, it is."

After a moment, she asks, "Do you remember the big whiteboard we used to have in the kitchen? Where would you write all of our big homework assignments and Second Chance's big events? You need something like that."

I lean my cheek against the top of her head. "That was a lot easier because I was always home. I can't take the whiteboard to school with me."

"You know what they say, Mom?" Hattie grins mischievously. At my quizzical look, she responds, "There's an app for that."

"Ha, I'm sure there is. It's one mistake, and it's not a huge one, so I'll be okay."

I go back to reading, and Hattie flips open one of my nearby notebooks, thumbing through my handwritten notes. Most of the students in my classes take notes on their laptops. I did sometimes if, say, I forgot a pen—where do they all go? I swear I restock every week—and was tired of having to ask my neighbor to borrow one. But all too often, I'd find myself browsing the internet or chatting with my friends, so I tried to take handwritten notes more often so I'd be less distracted.

Even now, reading about how perceived oversight by management changes worker production, I want to look up statistics of how much of manufacturing has been automated, but that would probably lead me down a rabbit hole to shrimp procreation or something equally irrelevant.

How did shrimp have sex? Or did they lay eggs? I've seen female crawfish carrying egg cases under their tails; is that how it works for shrimp too?

I close my textbook. Shrimp sex. I definitely need to call it a night.

17

Santo

Saturday morning, when I exit my apartment, I'm not alone in the hallway. Emma's door is open, and she stands in the doorway talking to an American man. He's wearing jeans, a collared shirt, and sneakers, holding a bouquet.

My eyes dart from the flowers to Emma to the man and back to the flowers, and something curdles inside me. "Good morning," I call in Italian.

"Santo, hi," Emma says, her gaze darting between us. She said the man who harassed her on the street was a local, so I don't think this is him. Plus, I doubt a degenerate catcaller would show up with flowers.

I take a few steps to join them. Emma didn't call me Professor Offredi; she called me Santo. Is that a signal of some kind? I offer him my hand. "Santo Offredi, a neighbor."

The man takes my hand. "Bruce Chance."

"The ex?" I frown.

His eyebrows raise, and his mouth turns down. Surprised that I've heard of you? Oh, I haven't just *heard* of you.

I could lean forward and tell this man that I've tasted his

ex-wife. That I know I could do a better job of satisfying her in one night than he'd done in years if she gave me the chance.

I glance at Emma, and she looks more worried than anything. I don't want to cause problems for her—especially given that this man is here to win her back.

What an idiot. I would say he has no chance, but do I really know Emma that well? Women go back to worse men all the time, and maybe I have an overinflated idea of how wonderful Emma is, but I get the impression that she doesn't think so highly of herself.

Someone should remedy that. The woman needs more support in her life if she thinks going back to him is a good idea.

I'm still shaking his hand, and it's been long enough that his gaze has shifted from cautious friendliness to concern. "What brings you to our city, Bruce?" I tighten my hand a bit because it feels good, a purely selfish act, nothing to do with how this man left Emma.

"I brought our daughter for a visit," he says.

"And you brought flowers," I add.

"Yes." He holds them up. "Perhaps we should get these in some water, darling." He firms his grip on my hand even more and gives it a shake, ending the standoff.

"Yes, okay, come in. Santo, I'll see you later."

Bruce smirks as I let go. "You deserve better," I say in Italian, knowing neither of them will understand. I say goodbye and leave them; the door slams, echoing down the stairs as I jog down.

I'm not an idiot. Flowers, history, three kids. A lot of reasons to try to make their marriage work again.

Anger bubbles up. What if Emma leaves the program? Leaves Italy? She came here to prove that she could do it without him, that she could have her own successes.

If she goes back to him, what is the likelihood that all of that will wash away?

A part of me is bitter too. While I am still friendly with Bell's mother, there was never a moment where I wondered if I should go back to her. It was not a disastrous divorce, like my first one, the kind where you end up hating each other and destroying everything good, but the kind of divorce where both sides realized there was no passion left.

And here Emma has a husband who's still got feelings for her, who is, maybe even as I think this, wooing her back.

They are not constructive thoughts, and I am reading a lot into a chance encounter in the hallway, but the thoughts exist regardless.

This puts me in a sour mood for the rest of the day. I run errands in the morning, then return to the apartment to change into my football uniform for the afternoon match. I ruminate in a stew of anger, worry, and a bit of sadness. Even Vincente comments on it Sunday afternoon over lunch. Emma has had all weekend with another man, and I am unreasonably cranky about it.

I don't see Emma or her ex at all until that evening. She's returning to her apartment at the same time I come back from dinner. Bruce is nowhere to be found, and neither is her daughter.

I get to the lobby door first and hold it open for her.

"Hi," she says as she passes, her eyes bouncing back and forth between mine.

Once we hit the stairs, I ask, "Did you have a good time with your daughter?"

Emma's face lights up. *Prosecco*, I think.

"It was so good! We ate way too much"—she pats her stomach—"and walked *a lot*."

"And Bruce?" We reach the top of the stairs.

"He was there."

A wonderfully ambiguous statement. I know I don't have

any right to ask Emma about this, but I do anyway, because I'm a weak man who can't help it. "He brings you flowers, flies in from the States. I think he had intentions, no?" We've arrived at Emma's door, and I lean against the wall next to it, crossing my arms.

"Santo—" A door slams upstairs, and Emma glances up. Stepping back, she gestures me into her apartment, and I follow. "He did have intentions," she admits after shutting the door.

My heart jumps. She looks hesitant, wary even.

"I have no right to this, I know. But he does not deserve you."

Emma raises her eyebrows. "You don't know me that well, Santo. We had one night together, and it wasn't that good." She laughs, but it's the sad kind. "That was my fault, I know."

"It wasn't your fault. So you have hang-ups. Lots of people do."

"You don't know my history, Santo. You don't know what my sex life has been like, you don't know the things that I enjoy, you don't know..." She hesitates, biting her lip. "You don't know a lot about me. It's pretty presumptuous to think I deserve some idealistic life."

"Don't say that!" I snap at her, anger rising. "Don't talk about deserve or not. Think about what you want in life, and ask yourself if Bruce can give it to you."

"God, Santo." She drops her hands. "I didn't even say I was going to consider it."

"You're not? You have a history and kids together."

"Are you trying to convince me to be with him or not?" She throws her hands out in exasperation.

I don't know *what* I'm trying to do. "I just want to make sure you know that you have options."

"I have options? Oh, really? What exactly are my options here? I don't have men banging on my door who want to have sex with me."

She could, I think, but bite my tongue. She's so much sexier than she gives herself credit for. If she went out to meet someone…

My hands clench, and my jaw tightens. There are enough men like Bruce out there, like the ones catcalling her on the street. I may not be the son my father expected or the husband my ex-wives wanted, but if I know one fucking thing, it's how to please a woman.

"If you ever think about going back to Bruce," I grit out. "Tell me."

"And what, exactly, will you do?" She crosses her arms and cocks her hip as if presenting me with a challenge.

"I'll show you exactly how good it can be myself."

18

Emma

Santo dropped that bomb on me, those gritted words spoken like a vow, and then turned around and stomped out my door.

"I'll show you exactly how good it can be myself."

Part of me is doubtful. I rarely orgasmed around Bruce for a variety of reasons. And, of course, it didn't start like that. But that is how it ends up, usually, when you've had kids and jobs and over twenty years of marriage.

Back when I'd started getting to know Jade better, I discovered that women my age really do have great sex. But Jade was single, knowledgeable, outgoing, confident...a slew of things that I wasn't. I'd done some searching online and wandered upon a forum called Dead Bedrooms, full of people who had marriages with unsatisfactory sex lives.

I saw post after post that could have been written by me— or Bruce. Maybe it wasn't *normal*, but it was happening often enough, and I related to it.

But there's another part of me, the part of me that replays Santo's words over and over again, that gets carried away imagining what being with Santo could be like. Leaning back against my door, I clench my thighs together, aching just from that simple sentence.

I was serious when I said I wasn't going back to Bruce. I will admit, there were a few moments this weekend with Hattie where it felt like a family again. Touring Rome, my gaze occasionally caught Bruce's as we both smiled wistfully at her enthusiasm, the unspoken *Can you believe we created this?* passing between us.

And then Bruce had shown up on my doorstep Sunday morning with the flowers and he'd taken me out to breakfast and proposed that we try again. That maybe "we'd" been too hasty in filing for divorce.

I had politely, but firmly, told Bruce no.

I wish I'd had a picture of his face to show my friends.

Words will have to do. I move to the couch and start a video call. Tessa might be traveling back to Portugal from visiting Luc, but Sara and Jade are probably available.

Sara answers first, her phone propped up on the counter in the kitchen. She teaches yoga classes online live on the weekends, but she dedicates her Sunday nights to meal-prepping.

She steps back and waves as Jade joins the call. Jade is on her couch, reading glasses on and a cocktail in hand. While we mostly drink wine together, Jade loves a good homemade fancy cocktail, so I'm not surprised by that.

We all say hello and then discuss Tessa's whereabouts, speculating if she was on her flight back from Paris or hadn't left yet. Or if she decided to miss it entirely and spend an extra day or two in Paris, which she has threatened to do several times. She works remotely for a travel magazine, so she can work from anywhere, but she usually chooses not to because Luc is "distracting," saying it in a way that makes it clear that they have lots of sex. How he can be "distracting" while living with his octogenarian grandmother is anyone's guess.

Before we can finish speculating, Tessa joins the call, and we ask about her weekend and tease her to her face about her eleven-years-younger boyfriend. She laughs and looks smug and not at all embarrassed. And then she diverts the attention to me.

"Was there a particular reason you called, Emma? Maybe something having to do with being MIA all weekend?" she asks.

"I was MIA because Hattie came to visit me."

All three of them coo.

"And Bruce came with her."

Dead silence.

Well, Bruce really surprised them—and me—when he asked for a divorce, so Bruce is two-and-oh now.

"Excuse me? Disculpe? Dǎrǎo yīxià?" That's Jade. She learned some Mandarin when she worked in Shanghai.

"Why did Bruce come to Rome?" Tessa asks.

I fill them in on the entire weekend, up to Bruce leaving but skipping over Bruce meeting Santo. When I describe the flowers he brought and the way he held my hand at breakfast as he asked me to reconsider our relationship, there's a variety of faces staring back at me. Jade looks bemused, Tessa pained, and Sara bewildered.

"I said no," I clarify.

Tessa's face relaxes, like maybe she was worried about it. Jade just says, "Of course you did," and Sara laughs.

"You should have seen his face," I tell them. "I really was pretty firm about it. He was surprised, and he kept saying I should think about it. He offered to help me with an MBA program in Austin. And, of course, he pointed out that I could see the kids more."

"I know that's tempting," Sara says. "And I'm not really one to speak about independence from your kids since I went all the way to Germany to be with mine, but still. I'm proud of you."

"You can do so much better," Jade chimes in.

"That's what Santo said."

Eyebrows raise. "You consulted Santo before us?" Jade gasps, mock affronted with a hand on her chest.

I fill them in on Santo's part of the weekend.

"'I'll show you exactly how good it can be myself.' Wow. That's…wow." Jade fans herself. "You can have an orgasm date!"

"I'm, like, ninety-five percent confident that I don't want to go back to Bruce. But there's five percent of me that's like… what if it could be better than it was before?"

"It's like Schrödinger's orgasm!" Jade crows. "Will it be better or worse? There's only one way to find out."

"Opening the *box*?" Sara snickers.

We all giggle until Tessa gets serious again. "Bruce had twenty-three years to have great sex with you," she says gently. "I'm not saying it wouldn't be a little better, but there's so much more to it than sex, right?"

"Yeah, and how much better could it be?" I ask.

"*A lot* better." This comes from Sara, and the rest of us go quiet. Jade has an eyebrow raised, and Sara blushes. "Well, I mean, Chris is pretty good with that stuff, and I had no idea how very good it could be."

"The man has made it pretty clear he wants to have another chance to go down on you, I think. What do you want?" Tessa asks me.

"I am very attracted to him. But he would be putting his career at risk. And I don't know what would happen to me either. It's not like I can walk into the offices and ask without raising suspicions."

"Santo is responsible for his own decisions," Jade points out.

Tessa chimes in. "I'm more worried about you, sweetie.

You ran out last time because you weren't comfortable. I don't want you to put yourself in a situation that you don't actually want just to spite Bruce."

"But this time, it'll be different," Jade argues. "Emma can be better prepared. Showered, shaved, whatever she wants. And it's premeditated, not a spur-of-the-moment thing. I think it's a good move."

"It could be risky for my career, too. What if the school or my classmates found out I was sleeping with a professor?"

"That's true. You'd have to be really careful," Jade says. "Sneak around. Lies of omissions, white lies, straight up lies. But you live down the hall from each other. Easy access." She taps her chin with a finger. "It's kind of hot, actually."

I roll my eyes. "Is there anything that doesn't turn you on?"

"Would you like to compare Yes, No, Maybe lists, babe?"

"I don't even know what that is."

Jade proceeds to give us a lesson in safe kink practices, and two minutes after we hang up the call, she sends us a PDF of her favorite list "just in case."

I'm still not sure what I'm going to do about Santo. It's not like me to do any of this—one-night stands or forbidden hookups.

But maybe that's a good thing.

19

Santo

THE WORDS I THREW OUT HAUNT ME. THEY WERE HONEST—*TOO honest*—but Emma and I pretend they didn't happen.

For my part, it was a totally inappropriate thing to say to a student.

Emma, though, is hard to read, but I suspect she doesn't believe me—or believe in herself.

She's out of town once again over the weekend, and so are Eva and Oliver, so I have a weekend playing football, working, and jacking off while having inappropriate thoughts about one of my students. But I'm also waiting, anticipating her return home, and wondering if she'll take up my offer.

She does not come by Sunday after she returns.

Monday, I don't see her until my lecture, and I'm sidelined afterward by another student's questions.

My disappointment grows. I had half-hoped that she would return eager to take me up on my offer. That doesn't seem to be happening.

The next week, Emma doesn't show up on Wednesday. After the session is over, I check my email, expecting a note from her explaining why she skipped my lecture, but there's nothing there. On Thursday she doesn't show up either, and I haven't seen her around the apartment building.

I'm getting concerned.

On Friday morning, I knock on Emma's door and don't get an answer. I knock on Eva's door and ask if she's seen Emma. She hasn't. I check in with the other professors throughout the day; same story.

I return to the building Friday afternoon and knock more insistently. While I wait, I pace the hallway. I call the landlord, and he hasn't heard anything.

What if something is wrong? What if she ran into that guy again, the one that followed her? I'm flooded with images of him being a sophisticated stalker who moves to kidnapping and serial killing, though the more logical side of my brain tells me that's highly unlikely.

I bang so hard on Emma's door that Eva comes out to check on me. She leaves Oliver inside, and we're discussing calling the police when there's a noise on the other side of the door, and I shush her.

A few excruciating moments later, the door opens, and I sag in relief when I see Emma. It's short-lived, though, because she looks awful. Her hair is a mess that possibly used to be a bun and what's come out of it is sticking to her sweaty neck and face. She's wearing a damp tank top with nothing underneath, cotton underwear, and a blanket like a cape.

Eva and I exchange a glance, and Emma blinks at us. "Emma," I say. "Are you okay?"

She blinks again. "Sick." She turns and stumbles toward the bedroom but then diverts course and crawls over the arm of the loveseat to lie face down on it.

Eva and I both step inside. I take off my blazer and crouch next to the couch. "Emma, piccola, what's wrong?" I place the back of my hand on her forehead. She's burning up.

"Sick," she repeats, her voice hoarse.

"I'll go get a thermometer," Eva says from behind me, and she disappears.

"Chills?"

Her head moves in the barest of nods.

"Body ache?"

Another infinitesimal movement.

I check her lymph nodes—swollen—and when Eva returns with the thermometer, I take her temperature—thirty-nine degrees. High, but not too high.

"What can I do to help?" Eva says after hovering over my shoulder for a few minutes.

"Can you check her fridge for some orange juice or a sports drink? She needs to hydrate. I'm going to call a doctor."

A moment later, Eva confirms that there is neither in the refrigerator. "Can you run to the store, then?"

Eva disappears. Oliver barks when she goes into her apartment and then when she leaves. I call my doctor and friend, Chiara, to see if she can make a house call. When I explain Emma's symptoms, she says she can swing by in a few hours, but until then, she should drink lots of fluids, have some tea with honey, and—if possible—a hot shower.

When I get off the phone, Emma's fallen asleep, and I decide not to wake her until Eva gets back. I open the window a crack to get some fresh December air in and roam around, picking up used tissues and taking a few dirty plates back to the kitchen.

Eva returns, and I thank her for running the errand.

"I bought some tissues, too, and medicine for cold and flu."

"Thank you," I repeat.

"Do you have this?" she asks, peering back at Emma. "I'm so sorry, but I have to walk Oliver and then I have a date."

"Yes, I have her. The doctor is on the way."

Satisfied, Eva disappears, and I close the door behind her.

I crouch down next to Emma's head. "Piccola, wake up." I touch her shoulder, and she opens her eyes groggily. "Sit up. You need to drink something."

She sits up with my help, throwing off the cape-slash-blanket. I crack open a bottle of sports drink, the kind with electrolytes, and don't let her stop until it's empty.

This time, when she lays back down, she splays out on the couch. A new sheen of sweat has slicked her skin, but she falls asleep easily again.

I wait for Chiara impatiently. Emma's phone is on the coffee table and won't turn on when I tap the screen, so I find the plug and set it to charge. Then I take the sheets off Emma's bed and, when I can't find another set, set them to wash and make the bed with sheets of my own. Emma's phone chirps repeatedly when it turns on; I suspect she has a few people other than me worried about her.

Guilt stops me for a moment, but I know Emma has friends and family who would worry about her and who knows how long it's been since her phone had a charge. She never even let the university know she was sick.

It all becomes a moot point when I tap the screen and it asks for a face ID. It's not worth waking her up over another hour or so of her friends' worry.

I sit on the floor against the wall with my phone, waiting. Emma coughs occasionally, a wet sound that makes me worry.

Finally, Chiara messages that she's here. I kiss her cheek at the building entrance and lead her up.

"How long has she been sick?" Chiara asks when she sees Emma, setting her bag on the coffee table.

"She was in lectures Monday and Tuesday, so maybe it started that night or Wednesday morning?" I guess.

Chiara gently wakes Emma and gets her sitting up. She checks her throat, her neck, takes her temperature again, and asks a few questions about how she's feeling. Pulling a stethoscope from her bag, she listens to Emma's breathing, and then taps on her back in a few places. Finally, Chiara sits back on her heels. I finally notice she's wearing pumps and pressed slacks, with full makeup and a nice blouse. I might have interrupted a date night.

"Emma," the doctor says. "You have pneumonia. Do you have someone that can take care of you?"

"I can," I offer. Well, I insist, but I keep my tone pleasant.

Chiara smiles back at me before returning to Emma. "Is there someone else you'd rather call?"

Emma hums, her eyes closed and I worry she might have fallen back asleep. "What day is it?" she finally asks.

"Friday night."

"Maybe Tessa?"

Disappointed, I pull out Emma's phone. Chiara moves to give me room so I can hold Emma's phone up to her face to unlock it. There are a ton of WhatsApp notifications, and I click on them to find missed calls from several people. There are new messages in chats, too, but I ignore them and click on the missed call from Tessa.

"Emma!" a friendly but sedate voice answers. "We were getting worried."

"Actually, it's Santo. Ah, Professor Offredi."

The tone immediately shifts to concern. "Is Emma okay?"

"She has pneumonia, unfortunately." I explain the scenario to Tessa, who makes all kinds of noises over Emma's welfare. "The doctor asked if she had anyone who could take care of her, and she asked for you." I'm pleased with how neutral the statement comes out instead of desperate for Emma to want my help.

"Oh god. We were just in Zurich together—did she tell you that?"

"No."

"We were all in Zurich together—that's Emma, me, Jade, and Sara, the same women there the night you, uh...met

Emma. Anyway, we spent a lot of time outside, going to the Christmas market and stuff. It was pretty cold, and with all the people and traveling, I guess we passed something around."

I grunt in acknowledgment.

"Sounds like Emma got it the worst," she continues. "Jade was out sick Tuesday but worked from home the rest of the week. Sara missed it entirely so far. My throat started getting sore last night. I don't think it's a good idea for me to fly."

I relay this information to the doctor, who agrees Tessa shouldn't travel.

"Should we call her family?" Tessa asks. "Maybe one of the kids could come take care of her. Or, there's Bruce." Tessa says it hesitantly, like she isn't sure Emma would want that.

Dear god, I don't want Bruce to come, and I doubt Emma does either. "If you want to call them, you can, but I'll be here taking care of her, regardless."

"You will?" Tessa asks. "Don't you have to teach on Monday?"

"I'll take the day off."

"But hopefully, she'll be much better by then," Chiara chimes in. She's been listening while she scribbles instructions down on a piece of paper.

"I guess that's the best thing then," Tessa decides. "And if my throat gets better I'll fly down on Monday. But call us every day. Video calls. I want to see how Emma is doing myself."

"Yes, I will."

We swap numbers and when I hang up, Chiara hands me the instructions and a prescription for an antibiotic.

"Looks like you'll be busy this weekend," Chiara says, switching to Italian. "Get this filled as soon as possible, and it'll help. How's your health? It's been a while since I've seen you."

"Good. I know I am due for an appointment. I'll call you when this gets sorted out."

"Excellent." The doctor turns back to Emma and switches to English. "Would you like a shower, Emma? It would be good for you."

Emma nods, and the doctor and I help her up. Chiara is a slight woman, so we decide it will take both of us to ensure that Emma doesn't fall in the shower. We wash her with her clothes on and I turn my back while Chiara changes Emma's outfit. Throughout it, Emma is soft, like a weak kitten. I want to wrap her up and press my lips to her forehead.

Finally, she's in bed—in *my* sheets—and asleep. Chiara says goodbye and after I check on Zola, pick up the prescription, and have Emma take her first dose, I settle onto her loveseat to get some sleep, the whole time worrying over Emma.

20

Emma

I DREAM ABOUT SANTO, BUT THEY'RE NOT NORMAL, SEXY DREAMS.
He's making me drink stuff, and though I'm pretty sure
there's a kink for that, it doesn't feel sexual at all. It feels
nice…caretaking even.

Also, I dreamed about a blonde woman. Again, not sexual
dreams, though she was definitely my type. They were both
there, and maybe that was a sex dream, and I just don't
remember details? I'm not sure, but if that's the case, it's a
shame. I'll have to think about it more later.

Like a sex dream, though, I wake up sticky and sweaty
and badly having to pee.

The having to pee thing is completely normal, obviously.
I've had three kids; when do I *not* have to pee? But it makes
me think of the weird dreams.

Otherwise, I feel better than I did when I fell asleep. I
swing my legs over the side of the bed. It's black outside my
window, telling me it must be nighttime, but I have no idea
what day it is. I'm also in different clothes. A shiver slides

down my spine, one that tells me my chills aren't completely gone, but I'm pretty sure I can make it to the bathroom.

I have to walk past my open doorway to get to the bathroom, and my eyes catch a flash of movement big enough to startle a scream out of me. Santo jerks up from the couch, eyes wild.

I've completely lost focus on my muscles and quickly retense, sinking to my knees on the floor while urging my bladder to control itself. I squeeze everything—including my eyes—tightly.

I will not pee myself in front of Santo. I will NOT PEE MYSELF IN FRONT OF SANTO.

In the other room there's a curse and a thump and then an even louder curse and a softer thump. I open my eyes to see Santo on the floor in front of the loveseat, his feet tangled in a blanket and his T-shirt twisted and riding up his torso.

I squeeze my eyes shut again.

"Emma, are you okay?"

"I have to pee," I rasp, which explains somewhat but doesn't answer the question—I *will* be okay if I can make it to the bathroom. I stand, squeezing my knees together and thank god that I've kept up with my yoga practice with Sara and Jade got us started doing Kegel exercises years ago and I had pelvic floor physical therapy after Parker was born.

Even with all that, it's close. I press a hand between my legs and run as best I can while still feeling like shit and clamping my knees together, and if a little pee comes out, well, worse things have happened, and Santo doesn't have to know.

Bladder empty, I don't want to put my underwear back on, but also, I'm just wearing panties and a shirt. With Santo in my apartment.

Maybe I wasn't dreaming.

I crack the bathroom door open. "Santo?"

He grunts.

"Can you close my bedroom door so I can change?"

There are a few moments of silence, followed by a lot of grunting and then the click of my bedroom door. I put proper clothes on. I have to sit down on the bed between steps as the adrenaline wears off, and I realize how goddamn *tired* I am.

Finally, dressed in pajama pants and a T-shirt—I attempted to put a sports bra on but got too winded while I wrestled with it—I open the door.

Santo is stretched out on his back on the floor.

I step over him and sink into the couch, too tired to have a conversation on my feet. "What are you doing?"

He grunts. "I think I threw out my back."

"Oh no," I say, while simultaneously sinking down onto the cushions. "Should I call someone?"

"No," he says. "This happened once before at a football match. I need to get up and move around." He sighs and lies there.

"Santo," I whisper.

He grunts again.

"Have you been taking care of me?"

I can't see his face from here because the coffee table is in the way, but Santo's bare right foot curls briefly. "Yes. How are you feeling?"

"Tired. Very tired. Was there someone else here?"

Santo explains that he called his doctor to come see me and when I offer to pay, he waves it away. He tells me he's been talking to my friends on and off, especially Tessa, and she's been sick but feeling better and is planning to fly here tomorrow.

"What day is it?" I ask.

"Sunday."

I groan. I slept the entire weekend away and missed half a week of classes. This is going to suck.

An alarm goes off in front of me, Santo's phone buzzing on the table.

"That's the alarm for you to take your antibiotics." With a lot of grunting—him—and protesting—me—he gets to his feet and retrieves my medicine and a glass of water. I gulp it down obediently, and he measures out two pills labeled Tachipirina for himself—an over-the-counter painkiller common here.

I wrap myself up in the blanket on the couch, inhaling deeply but not at all like a weirdo when it smells like Santo, and then notice there's a pillow here too. "Were you *sleeping* here?"

"Yes, I have soup. Would you like some?"

Okay, I guess Santo doesn't want to talk about sleeping on my couch, but that also could have contributed to his back pain—it's definitely not big enough for someone our size to stretch out on.

"Soup sounds great, thank you."

Santo heats a pan of soup and putters around while I doze on the couch. He nudges me awake when he brings two bowls over.

The smell of lemon and chicken hits me hard, and my stomach grumbles. "It smells delicious. What is it?"

"Avgolemono soup. It's Greek."

"Did you make this?"

"Yes."

We hunch over our steaming bowls. The soup looks creamy and there are herbs sprinkled over the top, and chunks of what I'm assuming is chicken floating. I blow on a spoonful until I deem it safe and take a sip.

Oh god, it's good. I'm thankful I haven't been that stuffy—though I would take blowing my nose constantly over hawking up colorful phlegm any day—and force myself to savor the meal. When the kids were sick, I usually heated soup from a can. Of course, if one person in our family got sick, it worked its way through the entire group, so that not only was I sick, but I was also taking care of four people in various stages of illness.

Also, I'm not much of a chef—not like Sara and Tessa, anyway. And there's not a lot of soup season in Texas, at least not like here. Last weekend in Zurich, it was crisp and cold, and we ordered takeout one night. Sara had found a vegan restaurant, and we all agreed that her truffled cauliflower parsnip soup was the best dish of the night.

But as delicious as that was, I like this soup better. It's not vegan, so there is that, but it's bright and lemony and creamy and is hitting the spot so well.

I have a second bowl, though I'm full in addition to the lethargy that already existed, but I stay upright long enough to check my phone.

There is a slew of messages: my friends being concerned for me and then Tessa updating them via Santo; my kids each randomly texting me as usual and then Tessa telling them in a group chat that I've been sick; and some of my classmates checking in on me, but mostly messaging about school work that is so long and overwhelming I have to put my phone down.

I refocus on Santo, who is cleaning up the dishes. "Thank you for taking care of me," I tell him. He pauses while drying a bowl and looks up at me. His face is so honest, his features so handsome, it stops my breath momentarily.

"It was nothing, piccola." He frowns, sets the bowl down, and walks over to me. He's moving stiffly, his back bothering him, but he still bends down to put the back of his hand on my forehead. It brings us so close that I can see the rim of darker brown around his irises, like a chocolate ring.

Santo's gaze darts over my face, eyes, lips, and back up to his hand. "Still a little warm, I think. Should I take your temperature?"

I shake my head, dislodging his hand. "I just want to sleep again."

"All right." He places his hand on his back and straightens. "I am going to my apartment to check on Zola. I will be back, though."

"Aw, Zola. She misses her daddy." I mumble as I rise to my feet. "You can stay with her. Sleep in a real bed."

He shakes his head. "Tessa will be here in the morning. One more night won't kill me."

"Okay." I pause outside my bedroom door. "Do you want to bring Zola over?"

He cocks his head. "You wouldn't mind?"

I shake my head and leave it at that.

———

AN INDETERMINATE AMOUNT OF TIME LATER, I WAKE UP TO voices coming from the kitchen and a rumbling noise coming from somewhere above my head. There's a soft weight up there too.

From the living room, Santo is describing the medicine I'm taking. When Tessa answers, I shift, telling myself I should get up.

That shifting dislodges the thing on the top of my head with a grumpy *meow* noise. When I sit up, Zola stares at me from my pillow. The rumbling has stopped, and she looks, as usual, put out.

"I could not keep her out of your bedroom," Santo says from the doorway. "I hope that was okay."

Tessa joins him and smiles. "Morning, sunshine."

"What time is it?"

"Eight a.m."

I raise my eyebrows.

"I took the first flight this morning."

"From Paris?"

"No, I didn't go to visit Luc this weekend since I didn't want to risk getting Anouk sick. But I didn't get it nearly as bad as you did, so I'm here now." Luc's elderly grandmother had a fall a few months ago, and Luc moved in to take care of her and save money so that he could visit Tessa more often and quit one of his jobs.

"Sorry, honey."

Tessa shrugs. "You look like you've gotten the worst of it—"

"Gee, thanks."

"—and I'll see Luc next weekend. Now, when was the last time you showered?"

I groan at the idea of getting this sickly sweat off me, and Tessa grins. "Thought so. I'll take it from here, Santo."

Santo looks at me, reluctantly apologetic. "I do have a lecture."

I wave my hands. "You've done more than expected for a neighbor. Or a professor." Again, the words feel like poor substitutes for what he is or, maybe, what he has the potential to be. Although, after nearly seeing me pee myself, he's probably changed his mind.

I cast the thought aside as something I need to think about later. Santo steps into my room, and I almost think he's going to touch me before I realize he's reaching for his cat, the giant black ball of fluff curled up on my pillow.

With her gathered in his arms, he holds my gaze and tells me to get well. Tessa and I both watch as he leaves my apartment.

Tessa turns back to me and claps her hands. "Okay, shower."

We step into my small bathroom, and I glimpse myself in the mirror. "Oh no," I moan. "This is what I look like?" My hair is a complete disaster, which is a real feat considering how thick it is. I have a bun that's lost most of its mass and has flopped to one side. I look sickly, and with shock, I realize that I probably looked even *worse* than this at my peak.

If Santo is still attracted to me after this, perhaps his standards are even lower than mine.

21

Santo

With Tessa here to take care of Emma, I only had to cancel half a day of lectures. I spend the afternoon at the university trying desperately not to wonder how Emma is feeling and obsessively checking my phone for an update from either her or Tessa.

On my way home, I pick up a to-go order of minestrina soup from my favorite quick-service place and message Tessa on my way up the stairs.

She greets me at Emma's open apartment door. "Emma's asleep on the couch," she whispers.

"I brought soup," I whisper back and hold up the bag. Tessa waves me in and puts the soup in the fridge for later.

The apartment is very tidy—Emma's bed has new sheets, and it smells like cleaning supplies and fresh air.

On the couch, Emma sits slumped over, mouth ajar, and the sound of heavy breathing reverberates in the space. A laptop sits on the low table, and a show is paused on screen.

I take a few steps over to the couch and carefully sweep a

lock of gray hair out of Emma's face and let the back of my fingers graze her forehead. She feels a lot cooler now, and she's not huddled under a blanket anymore.

I remember Tessa is here, too, and stand, looking away from Emma. "Do you need anything?" I ask, straightening my jacket.

"I appreciate the soup. Emma's kitchen is..." We both glance at the tiny space. "A tragedy," she finally finishes. "But I suppose one dines out a lot when one is in Italy."

"You are welcome to use my kitchen if you wish. I will bring a key by tomorrow morning before I go back to the university. Just mind my cat. She is...well, Emma can tell you about Zola."

"I might take you up on that. Emma might like some homemade American comfort food when she gets hungrier."

I nod and walk toward the door, letting Emma get on with her sleep and Tessa get on with her caretaking. Tessa follows a few steps behind.

"Santo?" she calls just before I close the door behind me.

I glance back. Her arms are crossed, and she's watching me carefully. "If you think—" She cuts herself off as Emma shifts on the couch, and we both wait until she gets settled again and her breath evens out. Tessa takes two steps toward me. "I don't know you, and some men like to take advantage of their position of power over women. If you hurt her, I will fly down here and meet with the dean myself, even if Emma won't. And *then*, Jade will come, and my destruction of your career was mere child's play compared to how well she will eviscerate you."

Tessa might barely come up to my shoulder and has impeccable makeup, a cute upturned nose, and generous curves that I'm sure many men appreciate, but the fire in her gaze and the glint in her eyes tell me she might enjoy my destruction too.

"However," she sniffs and tilts her chin up, looking down

her nose at me. "If you realize how truly amazing my friend is, you'll treat her right and give her exactly all the time, attention, and orgasms she deserves after a schmuck like Bruce." She narrows her eyes. "*Lots of orgasms.*"

And with that last word echoing down the hallway, Tessa closes the door on my face.

———

EMMA IS OUT FOR TWO MORE DAYS. ON THURSDAY, SHE'S BACK at the university and looking like her normal self again. Though she does occasionally become the source of an inordinate amount of crinkling as she pops cough drops like candy.

After the lecture ends, she approaches the front, notebook and pen at the ready. "Professor Offredi? Can we talk about the makeup work I need to do?"

Together, we review the assignments she missed. Emma jots down notes and bites her lip once I've caught up to today. "When do you need me to have this done by?"

"Next Monday?" I suggest.

The skin under her incisor turns white from the pressure before Emma releases it and smiles. "Sure!"

I groan internally. Emma is lying. I frown and rub my forehead, thinking. This is why you don't get too close to students. Hell, I haven't even slept with her, and I am tempted to give her leniency on her assignments.

Or am I overcorrecting? I'm not a harsh professor, and I like to think of myself as fair.

Except for propositioning Emma.

Enough time has passed that either she isn't interested—totally fair but extremely disappointing—or she is either so secure in her decision not to go back to Bruce that she doesn't need convincing or she's so secure in her decision *to* go back to him she doesn't need convincing.

I'll show you exactly how good it can be myself.

With Emma having been sick, my brain had gotten a reprieve from repeating those words over and over again, but now that she stands before me hale and healthy, my mind can't leave it alone again. What exactly had I been thinking? I was possessive just because the woman told me how disappointing her sex life had been in the past.

And now I can't decide if I am showing favoritism or overcorrecting and being too harsh.

This is yet another reason why professors and students together is an all-around bad idea.

Emma is gnawing on that lip of hers again, and I realize I am flat out glaring. I gentle my gaze. "When do your other professors have you handing in your make-up work?"

"One of my professors gave me until Friday, the rest next Monday. And, um, you know I'm flying back home for Christmas, so…"

So, she's trying to spend time with her family, and we've all given her enough to do that she'll be working full-time over the holidays.

But then she'll just be back in the third term. It was a hell of a lot of work to catch up on. I suppose if push came to shove, I could argue that she'd received an extension for all her courses, and what's the harm in an extra week?

"How about the Friday after that, then? Do you have colleagues who can help you?"

She nodded. "Shonda and I study together. She said she would help me catch up."

"All right." I realize, after all of this debating with myself, that I probably need to apologize to Emma about the proposition. But there's a knock on the door, and one of the faculty pokes their head in.

"We are on schedule for the OUT meeting in here, yes?" Professor Wang surveys the empty room and raises an eyebrow.

That's fine. An empty room at the university wasn't an appropriate place for me to apologize for propositioning her, anyway.

I apologize to Professor Wang and follow Emma out of the room.

"Anything else, Professor Offredi?" she asks once we are in the hall.

"No. Please contact me if you have questions."

Emma waves and walks off, and I'm left alone in the hallway, still berating myself.

When I get home, I change clothes, sit on the couch, and spend a fruitless few minutes trying to get Zola to curl up onto my chest like she always does. She refuses because I reek of procrastination and desperation, so instead I go knock on Emma's door.

"Professor," she greets me in surprise. She's changed for the night, wearing cozy pajamas and her hair up in a bun.

"May I come in?"

"Sure." She steps back, letting me into her little apartment, then folds her arms over her chest, right under her breasts, and leans her hip against the couch. Her place still smells vaguely like cleaning supplies, and there are books and coursework scattered over the kitchen table. "Is there a problem with the make-up assignments?"

"No, this is a personal visit. I wanted to apologize for my proposition to you the other week. It was out of line, and I want you to know that nothing will come of you saying no. I won't behave improperly around you at the university, and I will do my best to treat you like any other student."

Emma's gaze drifts over my shoulder, a small frown on her face as she thinks. "Did I say no?"

That's not what I expected, and I clear my throat. "Technically, no."

"What exactly did your proposition mean, anyway? 'I'll show you exactly how good it can be myself.' What does that entail?"

I pinch the bridge of my nose, having some choice words with myself in my head. Well, I guess I have, technically, licked her pussy. "One night. I would make you come any way you'd like. Finish what we had started."

"One night," she repeats. "And all you want is to, um, go down on me?"

"Yes."

"You would do that, even after last weekend?"

"Last weekend?" I am confused again. This has gone pretty far off from the straightforward apology and dismissal that I was expecting.

"Let's not pretend I was sexy at all while I was sick. I'm not sure why you'd still be interested after all that..." She trails off, casts about for a word, and then settles on "phlegm."

To be honest, I didn't notice anything unsexy about last weekend. It's not like I got hard listening to her coughing in her sleep or monitoring her fever, but it didn't change the way I think about Emma—this sexy woman who needs desperately, in my opinion, to ride my tongue.

I corral my thoughts back to the question at hand. "Yes, I would still be interested in that. I still find you unbelievably sexy."

Emma's cheeks go pink, but she looks at me skeptically. "Does that mean your offer still stands?"

This time, I rub my jaw, my beard rasping over my palm while I think about it. "Yes, I'm not rescinding it."

My heart, which realizes our conversation is getting somewhere interesting, is beating faster.

Emma studies me for a moment. "We have, I suppose, already technically done that before."

There's a glint in Emma's eyes that I haven't seen since the night we first met. I think she's flirting with me. Longing blooms in my chest. I liked the way we were together that night, without the professional relationship between us.

"Yes, we have." I shift on my feet and bring myself a few centimeters closer to her. Emma looks at me, her eyes wide and cheeks flushed. She licks her lips, and my gaze drops to her mouth. The scent of eucalyptus washes over me.

And somewhere, an alarm goes off.

Emma and I both flinch apart. She spins and digs her phone out from beneath a stack of papers on the table. "Sorry. I set a timer to try the Pomodoro technique to see if it would help me focus on my classwork. But, uh, you distracted me."

I look over the papers again, the textbooks, the open laptop. There's a small pile of cough drops and a slightly larger pile of empty cough drop wrappers next to it.

"You still aren't feeling well."

"I'm fine, really," she protests. "I feel a lot be—" She's interrupted by a wracking cough. She covers her mouth with her hand and the other falls to her abdomen, while she nearly doubles over from the force of the cough.

There is a glass of water on the counter, and I hand it to her. By the time she calms down enough to breathe and to drink, her eyes have watered, and her cheeks are flushed—not from arousal or embarrassment this time.

"I swear, I really am a lot better," she insists between gulps of water. "It's just this lingering cough that I can't kick."

I bite my tongue.

Once she's caught her breath, drunk the whole glass of water, and I've refilled it for her, I make a suggestion. "You're still"—I can see the protest forming on her lips already—"recovering and you've got a lot of work. We're not in a rush."

Finally, she nods.

"We'll talk after the holidays," I suggest. "Get your work done so we can enjoy ourselves."

I leave Emma's feeling like I've just given myself and Emma a reward for good behavior that I have to wait weeks to claim.

22

Emma

I DON'T HAVE A LOT OF TIME TO THINK ABOUT THE FACT THAT Santo still wants to give me an orgasm. He was right—I have a lot going on. I've been swamped with my schoolwork and, not that there's a great time to miss almost a week of school, but having been sick right near the end of the term means everything is crammed in at the last moment.

For Christmas, I go home to Texas. In the divorce, we decided to sell the house, and I was renting a place before I came to Europe, so now I rent an Airbnb for the week, and the kids fly back home. On Christmas morning, when I throw Pillsbury canned biscuits into the oven and watch some videos for my classes, the house is deceptively quiet. Long gone are the days of early morning furors of opening presents and playing with toys.

Parker comes down the stairs first. Growing up, they'd been the quietest of my three kids, and now that they are in college out west, they are really coming out of their shell...at least, I can't keep track of all their new friends' names and the

145

photos on Instagram make it seem like Parker is having a great time.

"You're studying," they observe once they've poured a cup of coffee and sat next to me. I wrap my arm around their shoulders, and they snuggle in closer, a warmth spreading through me I've been missing.

"Yes, well, falling ill and being unconscious for nearly a week is pretty detrimental to my coursework."

We fall silent as I click the link to an external source and read a case study on the Keynes Multiplier for my Macro Economics class.

The front door opens and Hattie bounds through, running gear on and drenched in sweat. It's a warm Austin Christmas this year, and while we debated celebrating elsewhere since we were renting a house, it was ultimately decided that we would stay in Austin. I wanted Bruce to be close enough to come celebrate but not stay in the same house or hotel as me.

"Merry Christmas," Hattie says, kissing my cheek and ruffling Parker's pompadour. Parker swats at her until she ducks out of reach on the other side of the kitchen island. She opens the fridge, pulling out some fruit and a sports drink while Parker settles back in at my side.

A few minutes later, which my children both spend scrolling on their phones and snacking on sliced melons, my phone buzzes next to my laptop. There's a new message on WhatsApp from an unknown number.

> Tessa gave me your number. It didn't feel right having hers and not yours. Also didn't feel right not wishing you a merry Christmas. Do Americans have eating contests with this holiday too? – Santo

I smile. Tessa had told me she'd given Santo my number when she'd left town, but this is the first time he's used it. I save his number on my phone, where WhatsApp automatically gives it his full name.

EMMA

No eating contests for this one. We cover a different deadly sin. Thanksgiving was gluttony, Christmas is greed. I spent way too much on Christmas presents this year. Call it post-divorce guilt.

SANTO

How very not-Catholic of you. Our neighbor, the Vatican, would pray for your soul.

EMMA

What are you doing for Christmas?

Instead of responding via text, Santo sends me a picture of Zola with a red bow on her head, the kind that has a sticky back so you can attach it to things. She is Not Amused.

"Who's Santo Offredi?" Parker asks, peering over my shoulder. I quickly flip the phone face down.

"Just a friend," I say.

"Wait," Hattie calls from where she's leaned against the counter. "Why does that name sound familiar?"

"I don't know," I say with mock exasperation. "Maybe I mentioned him before?" Whatever Hattie is about to say gets interrupted by the timer on the oven. Saved by the biscuits. "Your dad will be here in a few minutes. Can someone go wake Gabby up?" My oldest was out late last night catching up with her high school friends. Now that they are old enough to drink (legally), I expect she won't be trying to hide her hangovers anymore.

"Gabby!" Parker shouts from right next to my ear.

"Hey. Get your ass off the stool."

Parker takes two steps away from me before they shout again. It is a small house—two bedrooms we're sharing between the four of us—but still.

Hattie snaps her fingers. "I met him!"

"Who?" I ask while opening the oven. The biscuits are nice and golden brown, but the bacon still needs a few minutes.

"Santo Offredi. Your professor."

Oh god. How on *earth* did she meet him? Parker's head whips around like a dog scenting fresh blood. Behind them, the door opens, and Gabby stumbles out, sleepy-eyed.

"Who's Mom's professor?" she mumbles, making her way over to the coffee machine.

"Maybe if you weren't so hungover, you'd know," Parker taunts, putting their palm on their sister's face and shoving.

"Oh sure, *I'm* the troublemaker because I'm twenty-one now. We've all seen the party pics, Parker!"

This resolves into the two of them bickering, and then the doorbell rings and two seconds later Bruce is walking in. The kids greet their father, who's going to take them to visit his family this evening.

"Emma." He kisses me on the cheek. "Smells amazing."

"Thank you. Biscuits are done. Hattie, can you get the condiments out?"

"I want to make the moose snot!" Gabby calls out.

"Too slow," Hattie retorts from the open fridge.

Moose snot is a family tradition, one I don't even remember the source of. It's butter and honey mixed in a whipped bouquet of fat and sweet. It's a treat we only have on Christmas Day. The stick of butter has been out on the counter since I got up this morning, so it's perfect for mixing with the honey.

"He's cute," Hattie says.

"Who is?" Parker asks.

"Mom's professor."

"What? Let me see.

Hattie smacks their hand away from her phone. "You have your own phone."

"Enough," I tell them, but they ignore me.

"Who is this?" Bruce stands by Hattie's shoulder and leans over. This, Hattie allows. "Him?" Bruce's eyebrows rise to the stratosphere. "Your neighbor?"

"YOUR NEIGHBOR!" Hattie shrieks. "You live next to him?"

"Oh, Mom's blushing," Parker comments.

"Someone's got a crush," Hattie sing-songs.

"You should ask him out, Mom," Gabby adds. She's already pouring herself a second mug of coffee, so she's looking much more awake now.

"Maybe he's already asked her out," Bruce says, narrowed eyes on me.

"He's like, Patrick-Dempsey level hot. Like, stern brunch daddy hot," Hattie adds.

I don't want to know how she knows that phrase, which I only know from romance novels. But, uh… I should text that comment to my friends. Jade would be so proud, and also, it's accurate.

"Is he Italian?" Parker asks.

"Are you dating him?" Hattie persists.

"I'm not. Yes, he's Italian, but no, we are not dating." Technically, the truth. No dates have been had. Nor will they be had, for that matter. Santo might want to make my toes curl, but I'm pretty sure it's in the name of science. Or statistics. Whatever.

My kids throw up a chorus that's a mix of complaints and encouragement, and I never would have considered that they would have so many opinions on a guy they'd never meet. Or on my sex life. Maybe all the work Bruce and I do to be friendly to each other and demonstrate a healthy relationship is paying off.

"Are you dating him?" Bruce asks me quietly.

I hold his gaze, doing my best to look as honest as possible. "No, I'm really not."

"Okay," he says, raising his voice and clapping his hands. "That's enough. Your mother is not dating her professor and joking about it is how rumors start. If a rumor went around that a professor was sleeping with his student that could cost him his job, so let's not make a joke out of these kinds of things."

Ouch. True, but also a stark reminder that we should not be doing…whatever we're going to do.

But even as I think that, and as my kids get plates out and I pull the bacon out of the oven, a flutter of anticipation settles into my stomach.

Santo wants to do this regardless of the ramifications. He wants to go down on me *that badly*.

It's just one time, that's all. One time and I'll know what it feels like to be desired like that.

One and done.

23

Santo

Now that I have Emma's number, we text all the time. Vincente doesn't appreciate the pictures of Zola, but Emma does. After the first one she didn't respond for a while, but later she sent me a picture of herself with a very similar looking bow on her head and the message *we match*.

My Christmas was lonely, but I went over to Vincente's house for dinner, and I saw Bell two days ago to take her out to a nice dinner and give her a Christmas present—a Hermes purse I know she has had her eye on and another one to send back to her mother for Christmas.

I have a quiet week catching up on paperwork, which includes grading the last of Emma's assignments and giving her a passing grade. Next term, I have her in my Managing People and Organization course.

She's not back from the States until January 2, spending time with her kids for as long as she can. Vincente has me over to his house for a small New Year's party, where I ring in the New Year avoiding another guest who wants to come home with me, and then avoiding Vincente's questions about why I'm not interested in her.

She's forward and pushy and asked about my father. But I can't stop fantasizing about one particular blushing, prematurely gray, tall, and buxom woman whose pussy I want to eat.

The next day, just after lunch, I get a message from Emma. I do some mental calculations and it must be first thing in the morning for her.

EMMA

Happy New Year. I get back tomorrow.

I was wondering…does your offer still stand?

SANTO

Yes.

EMMA

Are you sure? You could get fired.

SANTO

I'm sure.

I know the risks I'm taking. I want this. And it's just one night.

What I don't say is that I need this too. Ever since the night Emma ran out, it's felt like an unfinished sentence. I tasted something and had it taken away from me, and I crave more of it.

EMMA

Your place or mine?

SANTO

Mine. Tomorrow.

EMMA

My flight gets in at 4. I'll be over around 6?

SANTO

Perfect.

I am hard all day thinking about Emma. Eva and Oliver are out of town for the holidays, and I'm not sure when they get back, but it means that I have no barking to accompany me when I can't take anymore and lie down in bed and stroke myself.

I don't miss it.

The anticipation doesn't abate, and I do it again in the morning before I head to campus. Emma is flying back, and I have meetings all day to prepare for the third term.

During the meetings, though, I'm distracted. So distracted that Vincente has to nudge me at the end of the meeting with the director. Snapping back into focus, I realize that everyone's rising and grumbling.

Shit. What did I miss?

I follow Vincente out and fall in beside him.

"I would not want to be Greco right now." Vincente shakes his head.

"Me neither," I agree, casting my mind back to remember what the topic of conversation had been before I'd gotten distracted. Something about the ski trip? Or one of the other club activities?

Vincente peers at me. "You have no idea what just happened, do you?"

I sigh, and Vincente shakes his head. "I don't understand what's up with you lately. If I was single, I would have killed to take Anna home. And when was the last time we went out for a drink?"

"You're the one with two teenagers and a wife," I point out. His son has been having some behavioral trouble, so it's not like Vincente has been keeping up his end of our friendship, either.

"Exactly. I could use a couple nights out with my best friend."

"So, what did Greco do?"

"He announced that a sponsor for the Ski Cup dropped out."

The Ski Cup was one of the main social events of the year where MBA programs met, typically in the Alps, for friendly competition and networking. I grimace. I have never been a big skier, but it's always been a popular event with the students.

Vincente and I chat more but part ways at my office. The sponsorship issue reverberates in the back of my mind for the rest of the morning, which is good because it distracts me from thoughts of Emma for a while.

Until my phone buzzes on my desk, and I glance at it. A text pops up on the screen.

EMMA

Just landed. Still on?

This constant checking to make sure I haven't changed my mind makes me chuckle and brings me back to my plans for the rest of the day. I text back immediately.

SANTO

100%, piccola.

EMMA

Just checking. :) See you soon.

I hurry to pack my bag and escape my office before anyone else can intercept me and put my mind anywhere other than Emma.

Back at home, I give Zola my undivided attention for ten minutes and then tidy up my apartment. I keep my work clothes on but shed my jacket and roll up the sleeves of my dress shirt. I have a glass of wine while I work, an oaky white that Bell got me for Christmas.

The knock on my door is early, but it's Emma on the other side. She's wearing the dress from that first night I met her, light makeup on her face and her hair braided over one shoulder.

"Hi," she says, cheeks flushed already. "I'm early, I kno—"

I tug her in by the hand, close the door, and press her against it. Her eyes are wide and bright, and I cradle her face in my hands. Nerves glimmer just beneath the surface of her gaze, and I vow to make this so good for her.

"I'm glad," I say, and then I kiss her.

24

Emma

THIS DIFFERS FROM THAT FIRST NIGHT TOGETHER. SANTO'S KISS IS careful, fueled by curiosity and not lust.

I'm glad he kissed me right away. I wasn't sure how we would get started; would we have awkward small talk over a bottle of wine? It didn't sound sexy. But neither did getting right to him going down on me.

But this *is* sexy. Santo doesn't press against me, but his hands hold my hips in a grip that tightens the longer we kiss. His mouth is warm and firm, a slight hint of wine but mostly the taste of him.

His lips are soft, sweeping across mine, his beard rasping against my skin whenever he moves. I shift on my feet, swaying closer, and he nips at my bottom lip. Just when I think he's about to deepen the kiss and involve our tongues, he pulls away.

"Which would be more comfortable for you: bed or couch?"

"Bed." The word comes out as a whisper, and I have to swallow my nerves and try again.

He plants another chaste kiss on my lips before taking my hand and leading me back to his room. There's a floor-to-ceiling bookshelf on one side and the only light is a bedside lamp with a warm glow. Opposite is a set of windows, beyond which the lights of Rome twinkle just like any other city. He guides me to perch on the edge of the bed and kneels between my feet.

Already? I lick my lips as Santo bows his head to press a kiss to my exposed knee.

"Just so you know…I trimmed." I gesture vaguely toward my crotch. "So, it's different." Santo looks up at me, eyebrow arched. "I didn't want you to be surprised."

"You thought I would be surprised that you shaved your pussy?"

I cringe. Even from Santo's mouth, with his sexy accent, that word is still so weird.

"What?" He rocks back on his heels.

"It's nothing." I wave my hand. "Ignore me."

Santo sits back even further, bracing his hands on the bed and not me. "If I say something you don't like, I want to know."

I stare at him, and he stares back.

"Fine. I don't like that word."

His eyebrows draw together. "Did I use it wrong?"

"No, you used it right," I assure him. "I just don't like it."

"What do you like? Cunt?"

I don't even have to say anything; he can tell I like it even less.

"Vagina? It's inaccurate, but I understand it is common."

I put a hand over my eyes. I can't believe we are having this conversation. "No, it's fine. I don't have a word that I like, so you can call it whatever you want. I shouldn't have said anything."

A firm grip circles my wrist and pulls my hand away from

my eyes. "I don't have to use any of those," Santo says gently as I meet his gaze. "How about figa?"

I repeat the word, and Santo says it again. It might be vulgar or insulting in Italian, but I wouldn't know. It *sounds* nice.

"Yeah, that works."

"Good." He rises on his knees again. "Lay back."

I follow his instructions, falling back onto the duvet. It's an off-white color, cool and soft.

A contrast to Santo's hands, which return to my knees, and his lips, which gently kiss the inside of my right thigh, just above his hand.

I close my eyes and focus on what Santo is doing. His nose nuzzles the spot he just kissed, and the air moves as he breathes in and out. His fingers tease the hem of my dress, his forearms nudge my legs further apart, he applies wet, sucking kisses. I pay attention to every detail lavished on me.

Oh wait…

I prop myself up on my elbows, looking down at Santo. "One more thing."

He raises his head. His eyes are hazy and hooded already, and I regret interrupting him. We hadn't even really started yet, but I *am* interrupting. That he is so into this already makes my stomach clench and my thighs twitch as I force myself not to clamp down in need.

"It might take me a while," I say. "If you need a break or to stop, that's fine. You know, like if your jaw or neck gets tired or something."

A beat passes before Santo speaks. "This is a good position for my neck," he says. "Better than on the bed together. And my jaw will be fine."

Is he trying not to laugh at me? Ugh.

I flop back, but Santo resumes his attention on me, and any lingering embarrassment vanishes. Instead, I'm hot and antsy for him to move up. Since I was sharing a place with my kids, I didn't masturbate at all this past week. Not that I do it often, anyway, but I thought maybe I should wait to be as horny as possible. And these past few days of anticipation certainly have me craving an orgasm.

When Santo first brushes against my underwear—just his cheek, I think—my hips lift off the bed involuntarily. He chuckles and turns, placing his open mouth on me through the silky fabric.

I groan at the heat, and then Santo takes a deep breath in, smelling me, and holy shit is that hot. He must like it because he does it again.

"Santo—"

His fingers climb my outer thighs and hook the side of my underwear, sliding them down. Cool air rushes in on me, but Santo is back in moments, his warm breath on my wetness.

"Che bella figa," he says.

Whatever it is, it sounds complementary, and I recognize figa. I didn't realize having a man whisper compliments to me in a foreign language would be so sexy.

And then his mouth is on me, hot and wet.

I hope he likes the way I taste. He seems to like the smell, so that's a good sign, right? And the trim…

Stop it, Emma. Focus.

Santo is definitely enthusiastic. I'm not sure what his tongue is doing half the time, but it feels good. He's experimenting, flattening his tongue, pointing it, licking different parts of me. I want to encourage him, but I also want to know what I actually like, so I try to relax.

After a few minutes, Santo's mouth leaves me. Oh no. I open my eyes and prop myself up on my elbows so that I can look at him. He leans back on his heels again.

"What are you thinking about?"

"I'm paying attention," I say quickly. "In the past, I've had a hard time focusing and I know that doesn't help, but I really am enjoying what you are doing. Am I not loud enough? I can—"

Santo cuts me off by squeezing my thighs. "Emma, you can think about whatever you want. You don't have to focus on me. You can think about a...a scene you like from your favorite book, or one of the Hemsworth brothers, or whatever gets you there. Whatever you think about when you are by yourself."

I don't tell Santo that last time I was by myself I was thinking about him. But what he is saying makes sense. I don't worry about Dream Santo noticing my flaws or getting tired.

"You don't mind?"

He laughs. "I'm the one between your thighs, enjoying your taste, so no, I don't mind. You'll just have to tell me which Hemsworth brother later." He winks.

This time, when he lowers his mouth, I cast about for something to think about.

A few years ago, Jade gave us a subscription to an ethical porn website for Christmas. We hadn't really talked about it since, but I kept my subscription going. I think about that now and remember one of my favorite videos.

A woman, white and blonde with a round face and soft body rides a man in reverse cowgirl. A lot of the scene was filmed from between his legs, watching her while she moves. Her being in control like that, the way she touches her own body while working her hips to move on his dick was the best part. His hands roamed over her body, too, but mostly it was her I enjoyed watching; the way she tweaked her nipples or gripped her entire breast in one hand and squeezed.

I do the same thing to myself through my dress and bra, though my boobs are bigger than hers and don't quite fit in my hand the same way. I leave one hand on my breast and let the other wander down, slipping under the hem of my dress to rest on my stomach.

Santo moans, and I squeeze my breast harder. In the video, the woman's partner eventually places his hands on her back, supporting her while she works herself on his dick. She bites her lip, her hips rocking and her thighs tensing. My body echoes hers, my hips moving against Santo's mouth, and he sucks on my clit. Heat surges in my lower belly, and I curl up. I can't hold it like that, so I move my hand on my stomach back and prop myself up on my elbow so I can keep watching, and Santo moves his right hand to my belly instead.

He alternates between teasing and firm, and so subtly I barely notice it happens, my focus is completely on Santo. I don't have to think about that video anymore because all I can think about is the way Santo's mouth is pulling on my clit and the tension coiling in my core.

"Right there," I gasp, and Santo keeps suckling. My whole body tenses up, my toes curl and a wave of heat washes over me. Then my head falls back, my body clenches and tightens as I come on Santo's tongue.

25

Santo

AFTER EMMA'S PULSES SUBSIDE, I SIT BACK ON MY HEELS. HER chest rises and falls, her pussy glistening with her juices. She hums softly and raises an arm to cover her eyes.

She might be self-conscious if she realized the view I have, so I drink it all in; the shortly trimmed hairs that cover her mound and the juncture where her thighs meet her center. She's pink and flushed, and her clit, which I sucked hard on at the end, is erect and begging me to take it in my mouth again.

Emma's breathing has evened out, and I wonder if she's fallen asleep. I press a kiss to her inner thigh, and she jolts. She lowers her arm and props herself up on her elbows, looking down at me.

"How was it?" I ask.

A broad smile blooms on her face, and then she laughs, falling back against the bed once again. "Fuck that was good."

I chuckle, pressing it into her skin.

Emma sits up fully, nudging my torso with her legs so she

can close them. I pull away and stand. She straightens her dress.

Emma's eyes immediately drop to my erection that strains the front of my pants. "Uh, do you want me to…?"

My lips quirk, and when she finally raises her eyes from my crotch, I shake my head.

I know I did the right thing when Emma looks at me skeptically. She can't quite trust that a partner would only want to give.

"But…" she gestures at my erection. "And this is a one-time thing, right?"

I lean down, putting my fist on either side of her hips and my face inches from hers. "This was a complete sexual experience for me. I enjoyed it very much."

If possible, she looks even more skeptical.

I kiss her instead of trying to convince her with words. If the taste of herself on my lips bothers her, she doesn't show it. Instead, her fingers run up the back of my head and into my hair, keeping me close, and her tongue meets mine.

This kiss is an echo of how we started tonight. It is the start and the end, a goodbye and a thank you.

When she pulls away, her eyes are clear, a spark of confidence in them that makes her even sexier.

"You were right," she says.

The kiss and lingering taste of her muddles my brain. "About what?"

"About how good it can be." She gazes up at me, clear and honest. "Thank you."

I slide my lips over and kiss her cheek. She stands and straightens the dress, then bends down to snatch up her underwear and stuff it into the pocket of her dress.

At the door, she turns to me. "I guess I'll see you tomorrow, Professor Offredi."

I rest my forearm on the door frame and lean against it, watching her walk away.

Perhaps Emma would expect me to jerk off when she's gone, but I don't. I flop down onto my bed and ignore my hard-on. The sheets, my hands, my mouth, everything smells like her.

I did the job. I can stop obsessing over a shy, blushing woman. She said it herself—I was right. It can be so good.

26

Emma

I don't know what to do with myself when I get back to my apartment. I've never had so little stress over trying to orgasm, and Santo made me feel sexy and didn't ask for anything in return. All things that should probably make me feel sad about my previous sex life, but the post-orgasmic hormones feel too good. What does one do after they have the best sex of their life?

Apparently, I have no choice, because once I pour myself a glass of wine I sit on my couch and replay the whole thing over and over again. I could pick up a book or take a shower or even pull the damp underwear out of my dress pocket, but no, instead I'm just going to smile into my wine glass.

Well, *eventually*, I pull out my phone and find a bunch of messages from my friends.

JADE

Tonight's the night!

TESSA

I think you are more excited about this than Emma is.

JADE

She deserves it!

TESSA

Of course she does. I'm just saying, someone needs to get some.

JADE

Shut it. You couldn't stay single if you tried. I know Luc is obsessed with that ass, but some of us don't have a reliable fix.

SARA

A fix??

JADE

There's nothing wrong with having a healthy sex drive.

Maybe the pussy eating skills were so good she passed out.

TESSA

A guy this confident is probably very good in bed.

JADE

As I always say...

SARA

Sex is 99% enthusiasm!

TESSA

It's 99% about enthusiasm.

SARA

Jinx.

I roll my eyes at my friends. They aren't wrong, but still.

EMMA

I'm here.

JADE

I need details.

EMMA

It was good.

It was really good.

JADE

Yes!! Go Santo.

TESSA

How do you feel?

EMMA

Surprisingly horny for someone who just had a good time.

JADE

Did y'all do anything else?

EMMA

No. But, he was definitely turned on. I offered.

It was staring me in the face, literally.

But he said no.

And it didn't feel like a brush off.

It was kinda sweet.

JADE

Cunnilingus doesn't have to be foreplay. It can be the main event.

EMMA

I know. And I don't think if I'd returned the favor I would be as floaty as I am right now.

JADE

Damn.

TESSA

Sigh. I don't see Luc until this weekend…

EMMA

Thank you for encouraging me. I think it was really good to be with him. I don't know if my expectations were so low, or Santo had such a casual and healthy attitude about it, but it was easy.

TESSA

I hope you still feel that way tomorrow when you're in his class again.

EMMA

He thinks it'll be fine.

I type this with more confidence than I feel. But Santo was pretty sure, right? He does this kind of thing more often. Well, maybe not giving his student-slash-neighbor the best orgasm of her life, but he has experience picking women up in bars and taking them home.

Our chat moves on to other things. We'd been messaging while I was in the airport earlier today, catching up on everyone's holidays. Tessa had spent it in Paris with Luc and Anouk. Sara and Chris had flown to Munich to have the holidays there with Zoe before packing her up and helping her move back to Austin now that her semester abroad is over. Jade flew out to Amsterdam for New Year's Eve.

JADE

Did we lose Sara?

EMMA

Maybe?

I think they are back in London now? Didn't they get an invitation to a New Year's party with some famous person?

JADE

'Some famous person'. Babe, you live in Europe now, you can't call Hugh Fetcher that. He had his own BBC show! He was on Doctor Who!

EMMA

Sorry I failed my crash course on British pop culture.

I've been listening to Verduistering.

JADE

I'm sure Chris appreciates being the entirety of your Eurovision knowledge.

Excuse me, I'm sure Chris enjoys his FORMER band being the entirely of your knowledge.

SARA

Chris says if you have to know one thing, Verduistering is still the best option, even if he's not in it.

JADE

Finally! Where did you go? It's okay if you had to sneak off and ride Chris's face.

SARA

I didn't ride his face, but otherwise you aren't far off, as little as I like to encourage your general assumptions.

JADE

Nailed it.

SARA

But now I have a private client.

Love y'all!

We all filter out of the chat, and I lean back on the couch, reflective.

Two years ago, I was in a sexless marriage, getting my third kid through school, and meeting my friends for drinks or yoga when I could. I never would have imagined any part of this life I have now.

I'm getting an MBA in *Europe,* and I had a mind-blowing orgasm from an extremely hot man, and then I told my friends about it.

This is me living my best life.

———

AND IT ALL COMES CRASHING DOWN THE NEXT MORNING. THIS IS why I shouldn't have hooked up with my professor because, when his class is the first of the day, several things happen.

My face goes completely red when I see him.

My legs clench together while I have very vivid flashbacks in class, which leaves my panties a mess and me unable to focus on anything else.

He treats me exactly like every other student, but I obsess about how he might not be looking at me as much or purposefully not looking at me at all.

I feel paranoid and needy all at the same time.

I remember his erection tenting his pants, and even though I told my friends I was glad it ended when it did, I realize I actually, desperately want to go down on him.

27

Santo

I have never been in so much pain in my life.

It's not unusual for one of us in the over-fifty team to have an injury, but this is the first time it's happened to me.

Sure, I have the usual aches and pains that we all experience, and my knees pop and get super stiff if I sit wrong, and there was that time that I fell at Emma's and strained my back.

This feels different, though, and it's bad enough that I had to call Vincente to come help me get off the football pitch and go home. It's been three weeks since the start of the new term, since I pleasured Emma, and now I have to live with seeing her every day. The mid-January air is chilly enough to send goose bumps up the exposed skin of my arms and legs now that I'm not running the pitch. I should have put my jacket on, but now it's too much of an inconvenience since we are almost home.

My team was in the middle of a game, and all I had done was look back at the player who had possession, a simple move of running while twisting my body, and next thing I knew, I was down on the ground in pain.

"Okay," Vincente says once we get into the lobby of the building, "almost there."

On the drive over, thanks to Vincente's urging, I called Chiara and she told me to lie down and ice my back and that she would come by this evening to check on me. The rest of her instructions were to Vincente, to make sure I didn't move too much and definitely couldn't lift anything.

The stairs hurt. Every step twinges my lower back.

"Should have taken you back to my place," Vincente mutters.

"Yes, I'm sure my addition to your household would be very welcome," I say through gritted teeth. Their house is too small as it is, but they've put up with it for this long, and the boys will be out of the house in a few years, god willing. Also, his wife is allergic to cats. "Mine and Zola's."

"That demon will survive without you for a few days. We could have gotten your neighbor to check in on her. You know, the hot one. What was her name? Starts with an E?"

I almost say Emma until I realize he means Eva. Vincente doesn't know that Emma is my neighbor. "Eva."

"That's the one."

I grunt. Eva is still dating someone, and hasn't been around much anymore. And Oliver goes with her, so things are definitely quieter here.

We have to pause at the top of the stairs for a break. I'm breathing hard and still sweaty from the match, although now it might be overridden by pain sweat. I'm not sure it should hurt this bad.

Now it's time to pass Emma's door. *Please don't be home, please don't be home.* Emma and I haven't had a private moment in these three weeks. We're back to a relationship where I'm just her professor and jerk off to thoughts of her in secret (when Oliver is not home). The difference is now I know how she sounds and feels when she comes.

I hate it. I got the closure I thought I needed. I know how that night would have ended, with the tastes and smells and the sounds. Instead, I'm wondering why I can't do that again and berating myself over and over for thinking it was a good idea. I still want her just as badly as I did before–no, worse.

"Santo, man, you need to breathe. Is it that bad?"

Emma's door flies open at the sound of my name. As soon as she catches sight of my face, her eyes widen. "Santo? What happened?"

"Ms. Chance?" Vincente asks, confusion in his voice.

Emma's gaze darts to him and then back to me. "Professor Romano." Then her eyes switch back to him, and she says his name again, surprised and actually seeing him this time. She clears her throat. "Professor Offredi. Are you okay?"

"He'll be okay. We're going to get him lying down," Vincente assures her. "The doctor's coming, but thanks for your concern."

"Sure. Okay." Emma steps back into her apartment, but the door doesn't click shut until we're almost to mine.

"Are you fucking kidding me?" Vincente hisses.

I wince even harder than I had before, which I didn't think was possible. Vincente's voice is angry and a bit hurt.

"Why didn't you tell me she lives down the hall from you?"

"It's not a big deal." I fumble with the keys and open the door while Vincente seethes. He waits to unleash on me until I'm lying down on the couch.

"Tell me she just moved in."

I sigh. "She moved in at the beginning of the program."

Vincente paces. "Where are your painkillers?" He retrieves them, and I choke two down. "Here's what I'm seeing. You took her home one night, ages ago. She moved in down the hall, which you never saw fit to mention to me. That's awfully suspicious. Why wouldn't you tell me?"

I close my eyes and put my arm over my face, waiting for the painkillers to kick in. "It didn't seem like a big deal at the time."

"Does it seem like one *now*?"

"Based on the volume of your voice, yes. Yell a little louder, and don't forget to enunciate so she can hear you."

"She doesn't speak Italian," Vincente points out. "And I don't want to know how you know what she can and cannot hear through the walls. She's two doors down! How loud have you two been?" His voice changes. "Oh god, there's an apartment between you. Eva. Does she know?"

"Stop," I snap. "You are blowing things way out of proportion here."

"Am I? I follow the rules, Santo, and even if it's been years since I've had sex, I don't act with my cock. Like father, like son."

He could have punched me, and it wouldn't have stunned me less. A chill washes over me. Vincente is the one person in my life who knows I have a half-sister.

"Fuck." Vincente's not looking at me but, instead, looks out the window. He's always been faithful to his wife, but I didn't know it had gotten so bad between them, and now I see our talks about the women I take home in a completely different light.

I close my eyes again. After a few minutes, I hear my friend move. The tap turns on in my kitchen, then off, and there's a soft clink as he sets a glass on the table beside me. Then my phone, and the rattle of the bottle of pills.

"Should I look for Zola?" he asks quietly.

"No, she's probably hiding up in her loft."

"Do you need anything else?"

Because I'm going to leave before you disappoint me even more.

"No."

A few moments later, the door clicks closed, and I'm alone.

28

Santo

I COME TO CONSCIOUSNESS WITH ZOLA ON MY CHEST, PURRING.
That's not what wakes me, though—my phone buzzing on
the table does. It's Chiara.

"Yes?"

"I'm downstairs. Can your friend let me in?"

"He left. Hold on." I try to rise to sit and grunt in pain.
Zola yowls in displeasure and hops off my chest.

"What about Emma?" Chiara asks.

"I'll figure something out. See you soon." I hang up. I have
a series of concerned messages from Emma and instead of
answering, I call her and explain the situation.

"Of course," she says. "I'll be right over."

I lay back and wait for the women to arrive. Zola tries to
climb back onto my chest, but I brush her off. I'm not in the
mood for a cuddle and I'll just have to push her off again
soon.

Like father, like son. I can't believe he'd fucking say that. I'm
a professor, for fuck's sake, not some egomaniacal import

magnate with two children, one that he completely ignores and hides.

But I have an unprofessional relationship with Emma. I took her home, I kissed her, I've made her come on my tongue. It's not the same, but is it really that different?

I'm pretty riled up by the time the women arrive. "Two house calls in as many months to this building. Stop trying to pay my bills, Santo," Chiara teases, but I just grunt at her. Emma hasn't said a word, but I can sense her moving around the apartment.

Chiara asks me a bunch of questions—did I stretch? What, exactly, did the pop feel like? Could I sit up?—and I am very aware of Emma hovering behind the couch. It reminds me of my mother hovering over my father when he was in one of his moods, and makes me even more irritated. My jaw is aching.

"How's your pain on a sca—"

"Emma," I interupt. "Can I have some privacy? Please?"

"Of course," Emma says, her voice quiet. A moment later, the door clicks closed.

Chiara stays quiet while she checks my vitals and tests the muscles in my lower back. She hums while she works, her fingers poking and prodding sore muscles. Then she makes me sit up and tests my reflexes. "No nerve damage," she comments, before rising to her feet and walking over to my kitchen to wash her hands. "Scale of one to ten," she asks me in Italian this time. "How bad is the pain?"

I have enough hubris to know that there is worse pain in the world, I've just never experienced it, not having the proper anatomy (or desire) for childbirth and never allowing my ex-wife close enough to kick me in the balls when she was in a peak of rage. I settle on six.

"You've got a lumbar strain. Some of your muscles have spasmed, which is causing the pain. You need to rest and ice your lower back. Since you sent my assistant away, and perhaps she wouldn't be able to handle the language barrier anyway, I'm going to go get this prescription filled." Chiara eyes me in disappointment, and I think it's quite the feat to get that sort of disapproval from someone who's at least two decades younger than me. "You helped her a lot when she was sick. Why can't she return the favor?"

"This isn't couples counseling," I bite out. I'm being an ass. I know it. Chiara knows it. Emma, from her apartment two doors down, definitely knows it.

"Someone is being a grumpy ass," Chiara reprimands like she's inside my head. "I'm getting your prescription. Consider this a time out and think about what you've done."

She departs, but instead of doing anything productive, I get lost in thoughts about my father until I fall asleep.

29

Santo

Of course, the moment I wake up, I feel like a shit for being so awful to Emma. However, it takes me until the next evening to feel like I can hobble over to her apartment and properly apologize. Fortunately, I have a bottle of Prosecco on hand; an apology gift.

At my knock, Emma opens the door and, despite the twinge in my lower back, I straighten and try not to grimace when I say hello.

Emma's eyes are full of sympathy. "How are you?"

"I have been better. Here, this is for you. I am sorry for the way I behaved. I should not have yelled and taken out my anger on you." I hold out the bottle of Prosecco, and her eyes soften even further. Am I ever going to think about Prosecco without thinking of her?

Emma takes the bottle. "Come in. I think we should talk."

I gingerly step inside, and she closes the door behind me. She's been working on her couch, notebooks and papers spread over the low table. There's already a glass of wine next to her laptop.

The fridge door closes, the bottle I gave her set to chill, and Emma leans against her little kitchen counter. "Why were you so upset at me?"

I rake a hand through my hair. "Vincente—Professor Romano, I mean, was upset with me for not telling him you lived in my building."

Her eyes widen. "You hadn't told him?"

"No." I look out the tall window and study the view of the building directly next door. All I can see is brick—very different from my view.

"But he knew about us?"

"Yes, but not…not *details*. I told him at the start of the term that nothing had happened, and I told him yesterday that nothing is going on between us, which is a lie of omission. But he didn't really believe me and made some accusations."

"So, you were upset that he accused you of sleeping with me?"

I look at Emma, finally. Her brows are drawn together, and I can see the self-consciousness warring with her desire for self-protection.

"I was upset," I say carefully, "because he said I was just like my father."

The wrinkle between her eyebrows deepens. "That was an insult?"

"My father had an affair with his young, naive secretary who got pregnant. Most people don't know about it because my father threatened and bought off the woman, but I told Vincente, and I was upset that he was right. I don't like the comparison, but I don't blame him for making it."

Emma's mouth purses. "That's bullshit."

"What is?"

"He wasn't right. You aren't like your father."

I snort. "You didn't know my father."

"Okay, fine, but here are some differences that I know." She holds out a finger and starts counting. "One; you aren't married. I'm pretty confident in this since I've met Abelie, and she would have said something. Two; how young was this secretary? I'm probably twice her age."

"Twenty," I admit.

"Three; I am not naive."

I raise an eyebrow, and Emma flushes before lifting her chin. "Maybe I'm inexperienced with some things, but I am not naive. I've been married, had kids, started a business, and got divorced." She sniffs. "I'm worldly now. Four; I can't get pregnant."

My other eyebrow joins the first.

"I had a procedure after kiddo number three," she explains. "Five; while you could certainly make my time in the program difficult, having an illicit affair with someone you depend completely on for your job is different. There are procedures in place to handle student discipline; you can't unilaterally fire me. Need I go on?"

I know Emma is trying to make me feel better. She stands there with her hand in the air, fingers outstretched, a flush on her cheeks.

But there's a part of me that hopes that she's making this argument not just so I'll feel better, but to talk us into doing something more. Even thinking that she might fight for us this fervently has my heart racing.

I am so fucked.

30

Santo

CHIARA CUTS ME OFF OF THE PRESCRIPTION PAINKILLERS, AND I make do with over-the-counter pills. I'm still stiff and sore, and in my worst moments, I wonder if I'll ever play football again. It seems unlikely when I'm still coming back from the university aching and spending whole evenings on the couch.

Vincente and I are not talking.

Bell came by to check on me last night, declared me "mopey," and cooked me dinner.

Tonight, though, I grit my teeth and climb the stairs. It still hurts, but Chiara says it'll get better if I keep moving.

When I reach the top of the stairs, my eye catches on Emma. She's sitting outside her door, on the floor, back propped up against the wall.

She's already blushing. I stop at her feet and look down at her.

"Are you okay?"

"I, uh…locked myself out. Probably."

I raise an eyebrow. "Probably?"

"Well, I can't find my keys, and I'm assuming they are

inside the door. It's also possible I dropped them somewhere. Or that they are, in fact, in my bag but I can't find them. Which has, unfortunately, happened before. Don't worry, I've called the landlord."

"I see."

I should invite her to my place to wait, but I am grouchy and miserable, and I worry I'll snap at her, and then I'll have to apologize *again*.

But I'm still tempted. I think part of me just wants to spend more time with Emma, and honestly, that side of me can fuck right off. It's hard enough to see her in passing at university and to hear about her, even off-handedly, from the rest of the faculty and to have moments like this one, where we're essentially at home, and she's still invading my thoughts.

"Good luck," I say, perhaps with a bit more curtness than she deserves. Whether Emma notices or not, she gives me a chipper, "Thanks. Have a good night," and I retreat to my apartment.

Zola greets me at the door with a meow, waiting impatiently for me to put my things down so I can properly greet her. Because of my back, though, I don't bend down to pick her up, and after a few minutes, she storms off in a huff to her loft.

I change clothes and pour a glass of wine. There's a football game on tonight, Roma versus Atalanta, that I plan to watch.

Mario, the landlord, won't take long to get here with a set of keys, right? Emma's in the hallway, not stuck outside where unscrupulous men might make her uncomfortable.

I recline on the couch, cushions supporting my lower back with my phone in one hand, glass of wine in the other, planning to catch up on emails and whatnot. Eventually, Zola joins me in her usual spot on my chest, and I ignore her, just how she likes it, and soon she's purring and face planted.

About two sips into my wine and five emails down I give in. Sighing, I sit up, dislodging Zola, who makes her displeasure very well known. My back complains too, but tough shit.

I'll just peek my head out. Maybe Emma's not even there anymore.

Except I do, and she is. She looks up at me and gives me a tentative smile.

"Would you like to come in while you wait?" I ask.

She hesitates, and I feel less alone having debated the offer if she's debating accepting. "Are you sure?"

"Yes."

Emma gathers her things, shoving most of it back into her bag but leaving two spiral notebooks on the floor— she'd unpacked quite a bit, perhaps in another attempt to find her keys. With an audible "oomph," and her other hand pushing against the wall, she gets on her feet, wincing.

Her knees didn't pop like mine do, but I know the feeling. She wiggles a bit, which does something quite nice to her breasts in her blouse, and when she catches me watching her, she blushes. "My butt fell asleep."

I'm awash in guilt. By trying not to tempt myself, I've let her sit out for far too long. Damned if you do, damned if you don't, I suppose.

Emma bends down to pick up the last of the notebooks and holds them while I lead her into my apartment. When I close it, our gazes catch, and we're face-to-face in this small entryway.

Months ago, in another entryway, I was on my knees. More recently, she was here on my bed, crying out while I ate her pussy.

Emma might be thinking the same thing because her eyes widen and her lips part. I can nearly taste her again; it's such a thick memory.

And then Zola jumps off the couch and runs through the

main room up to her loft, breaking the moment. I step back. "Would you like a glass of wine?"

"Please," says Emma. She sets her bag on the floor and the notebooks on my kitchen counter. I almost ask what kind she wants—I have two more open in the fridge—but refrain. It's too much like that first night, comparing her to wines. I pour a glass of the same wine I'm drinking and turn back to Emma. She's looking at a framed photograph on the wall, a picture of me and Bell at her university last year.

"How's Bell?"

"Good. She was here last night."

"That's nice," Emma remarks. "The worst part about coming here was seeing my kids less. They're in college, and only one of them is in Austin, so it's not like my ex-husband sees them more, but still. I no longer am the place for laundry and a hot meal."

I give Emma the glass of wine and return to my spot on the couch. She doesn't sit with me but wanders the room, looking at my things. I don't think there's anything terribly interesting—old textbooks on the table, more photos on the walls, and the view out the window.

"There's a football match—our football, your soccer. Would you like to watch it with me?"

"The only thing I know about soccer is the red card and the 'gooooooooaaaaalllll,'" she says with a smile. "Is it the same here?"

I tilt my head back and forth. "More or less." I turn the television on to the pre-match show and Emma joins me on the couch, finally.

After a few quiet moments of wine sipping and watching the TV, Emma speaks up. "I know you play. Is that how you got injured?"

"Yes." I explain the strain and how I'm still recovering, but there's not much to do but rest and let it heal. I don't voice my concerns that I might not play again.

Emma frowns. "Soccer—I mean football—is a fast game. How do you keep up with other players? No offense," she adds quickly, "but you are, um…"

Amused, I put her out of her misery. "I play on the over-fifty team," I allow. "But it is still a tough sport."

"Oh, right. That makes sense. Like how there's age levels for kids. I can imagine it would be hard to compete with a twenty-year-old." She pauses in thought. "I don't work out much. Sara, my vegan friend?" I nod. "She teaches yoga, so I do her classes to keep somewhat healthy. Though you won't catch me running." She sips her wine as the players walk into the stadium, holding hands with young kids. "Do you play offense or defense?"

When I tell her I play winger, she looks at me blankly, so I explain the positions and by the time that's done, the match has started, so then I teach her how football works. I'm sitting up, pointing out various moves and players on the screen, when Zola graces us with her presence. She winds around my shins while I'm explaining penalty kicks, and then she gets up on her hind legs, front paws on my knee, and meows at me.

I know what she wants, so I sit back on the couch and let her climb up onto my chest. I run an absent-minded hand over her back once she's in place and purring.

"Huh, that explains it," Emma says.

"Explains what?"

She gestures in a wide circle toward Zola. "Your white shirt had black hairs on it right at the center of your chest, and now I see why."

I look at Zola, who's put her face down already so I can only see the back of her head and her ears.

"What's happening now?" Emma asks, and I return my attention to the match. Emma asks good questions, and seems to respect the game, for an American. She's halfway through her glass of wine, and the smell of it and her is making me think about the night I met her.

Best to think about something else, especially with Zola in my lap.

We're twenty-three minutes into the first half when there's a slam next door and soft little yips come through the wall. Oliver is home. Zola lifts her head and her ears spin, contemplating whether or not she should complain about the noise.

Emma and I share a glance.

"Do you like dogs?"

Do I like dogs? Sure. Do I like Oliver? No. That little bastard barks every time I get my dick out, so no, I'm not a fan. I will not tell Emma that, though. That would cross a line.

"He scared you into pepper spraying me," I say instead. The words are definitely bitter, but I suppose being pepper sprayed is enough to justify it, even if the little shit wasn't the one pulling the trigger, and instead it was this bright, beautiful woman.

Emma chuckles. "True. I think it's fair to hold a grudge, then. He barks a lot. Especially when..." She trails off, and then a flush spreads over her neck and cheeks.

"Especially when what?" I ask, though I already have a guess.

31

Emma

I stammer. My cheeks are on fire, and Santo stares at me intently. "I...I...."

"Especially when what?" he repeats. His eyes narrow on me from behind his glasses.

Why, oh, why did I have to say that? Why am I such a hot mess that I can't keep track of my goddamn house keys? Why did I even take Santo up on his offer?

My mind goes completely empty except for euphemisms for masturbation. Flicking the bean. Paddling the canoe. DJing.

God, Jade would be so proud.

Surely, there must be some reason for a dog to bark other than that the neighbor is masturbating.

Why do dogs bark?

Santo must have had enough of me gaping at him like a fish because he shifts in his seat, the ball of black fur on his chest not even twitching, and strokes his beard. "I have noticed that Oliver doesn't seem to like certain activities that I do."

Certain activities. Oh my god. Does he mean what I think he means?

If I think about it...surely Santo jerks off. And oh dear god, now I'm thinking about it.

When Santo came out into the hall to invite me in, he was dressed casually; cotton lounge pants and a white V-neck T-shirt. Except for his soccer uniform, Santo has always been crispy dressed whenever I've seen him—his standard outfit is slacks and a button-up and a nice jacket. Even now that I've had months in Rome and have gotten used to a more European fashion sense, Santo is starch and polish and expensive, even.

So it's fairly surreal to be sitting on his couch with him dressed down and us even possibly, maybe, talking about masturbation. Even though he's used his mouth on me and made me cum gloriously.

I can't decide which I like better: Marlon Brando Santo or this Tight White Shirt Santo. Either way, I get pecs and chest hair, for Christ's sake. But my eyes involuntarily flutter when I remember that he's seen much more of me—he's been *down there.*

"Certain activities," I say, and I hope it comes out curious, but I suspect it's breathy.

"Yes," is all he says back. He's still watching me, eyes unreadable.

I startle when my phone chimes on the arm of the couch. Quickly, I pick it up and swipe the screen to see that Mario is here. I wave the phone. "Back to my apartment," I say, jumping to my feet. "Thank you for letting me come in while I wait."

Santo moves to dislodge Zola, and I hold out my hands. "No, it's fine. I'll let myself out. Let her sleep, and enjoy the game. Again, thank you."

"You are welcome."

I grab my bag and sweep out the door.

THE LANDLORD LETS ME BACK INTO MY APARTMENT. I'D BEEN texting with my friends while sitting in the stairwell, and now the conversation has moved on to Zoe's spring break plans. Apparently, she wants to join us on our next weekend together, and after talking it out, I'm exhausted and ready for bed.

I lay in bed for a few minutes. It's still early by Italian standards. I heard Eva and Oliver go out for their nighttime walk a little while ago, but all I hear now is the noise of the city streets, the hum of cars and people echoing off the alley walls outside my window.

Santo has been at the top of my mind ever since I sat on the couch drinking wine with him. I had another glass while texting with my friends, and now, lying in bed, I think about how there's an apartment between us, but he's probably doing the same thing I've been doing; a glass of wine, getting ready for bed—maybe he's even in bed. All while alone, separated by a small space.

What if he meant masturbation? If I were thinking, *What Would Jade Do?* I'd be putting on something sexy, gathering a bottle of wine, and heading over to ask Santo what he was talking about.

I'm not Jade. But despite my awkwardness earlier, I'm not just going to let it go. I don't think I can.

A door slams next door. Eva and Oliver are home.

With a silent apology to Eva and everyone else who gets disturbed by Oliver, I open the drawer in the table next to my bed and pull out the Magic Wand. Amongst my friends, we've nicknamed this one the Handy Man because it gets the job done, and it's definitely the easiest toy for me to use, even though I balked at it at first. It's so big and noisy.

My sleep shorts and underwear are gone in one shove,

and I spread my legs. Resting the head against my lips, I push the power button.

My toes curl right away. It's so powerful, even on the lowest setting. I've never gone beyond the second level, but I don't even think I'm going to need that tonight. It takes maybe twenty seconds for Oliver to start up.

Eva shouts at him, and I turn the Handy Man off.

Oliver's slower to settle than he is to get riled up, but she gets him calmed down soon enough. I lay in the dark tension ratcheting up as I wait, listening hard, as if I would miss it.

Just when I'm about to give up, Oliver barks again.

Oh my god.

I think…I think Santo is jerking off, just down the hallway. Pressing the button, I turn the Handy Man back on, holding it harder against myself and straining. I'm imagining Santo's face, the only part of him I've seen when he's aroused, the warm olive skin, his eyes closed in pleasure, and the lush, dark eyelashes against his cheek.

At some point, Oliver stops barking, but I hardly notice. The vibrator is still thrumming between my legs, and the tension in my core is building. With a gasp, I come, arching off the bed and pulsing on nothing.

When it finally passes, I flop back on the bed, laughing. That was the fastest I've come in ages. And to think it was just the *idea* of my professor a few doors down, maybe, possibly, also getting off that got me there.

32

Santo

THIS IS A DISASTER. THREE NIGHTS LAST WEEK I MASTURBATED TO Oliver's barking. Sometimes, he barks when I know Emma's not home, but I get hard anyway. If I'm not careful, I'm going to have a Pavlovian response to a dog's bark: an instant erection every time I hear one.

I do not know if Emma's reciprocating on the other side, but I think about it constantly. In fact, I'm thinking about it so hard right now that it takes a minute for me to notice someone's knocking at my office door, and based on their insistence, they know I'm in here, and it's not the first time they've knocked.

I clear my throat. "Come in." It's Monday, the last week of the third term, and it's been hectic with the coursework and grading. Not a good time for me to be off my game, and I half think that maybe it'll be someone complaining about my mental state or reporting that I've made a grave error.

To my surprise, it's Vincente. We haven't talked since our fight and have been avoiding each other.

"Hello," he says, lingering in the doorway, awaiting an invitation.

I gesture at the chair and close my laptop while he settles into his seat.

"How are you feeling?" he begins.

"Better. No more painkillers now, and I'm stretching every day."

"Good. Not back to playing yet?"

I shrug. Playing football is my way to stay in shape, burn off energy, and enjoy myself. At my age, my father was portly, smoking, and had a lot of stress in his life—not only his business but his continued affairs and his strained relationship with me and…well, everyone in his personal life. My back is a lot better, but I'm not entirely optimistic about being able to go back to my favorite sport. I might have to take up something else—biking or swimming—to stay fit.

He grunts in sympathy and picks at a bit of fuzz on his pants leg. "Listen, I owe you an apology. I know that if you were sleeping with a student, you would tell me. Right?" He looks up, meeting my gaze and frowning. He didn't actually apologize, nor is he confident in his own assessment.

With a sinking feeling, I realize he shouldn't be. I crave Emma so badly it aches, and that's not going away. We're nearly through the fundamentals terms, and nothing has changed.

I have two choices to stay above board—leave Emma alone or quit my job.

I don't want to quit. Teaching is a way to prove to myself that I'm not trying to live up to my father's standards anymore; I'm no longer trying to impress him, even after his death. This independence is important to me.

"Right," I say, and the lie is bitter.

Vincente and I move onto other topics, and when he leaves, I attempt to go back to work. But my mind wanders to my other option—leave Emma alone.

Could I do that? Should I pack up my things and move again to a different apartment, one where I wouldn't see Emma in the halls and on the commute to work? One where I wouldn't hear barking at night and wonder if she's touching herself. I could file a request to drop a lecture for the fourth term so I wouldn't be teaching her. I could swap with another professor and pick up an undergraduate course instead.

It niggles in the back of my mind for the rest of the day, though I bury myself in my work, lecturing and consulting with the CEO of a solar company. Back in my apartment that night, I attempt to work on my book, which has been languishing. My laptop is in my lap, and Zola is on my chest.

Until, that is, Oliver barks, and my whole body tenses.

It's late enough that I know we're all home—me, Emma, and Eva. Eva shouts, "Shut up, Oliver!" but he keeps barking.

I jackknife up, surprising Zola and causing her to dig her claws into my chest before she leaps straight into the air. When she lands, she rockets up the stairs to her loft.

I have to know. I *have* to know.

Five seconds later, I'm banging on Emma's door. I rest one hand on the top of the door frame and close my eyes, picturing her scrambling off her bed, putting her clothes back on, and hustling to the door. When it opens, I'm rewarded with exactly the view I was hoping for: Emma is flushed, disheveled, the strap of her tank top sliding off one shoulder, and her nipples straining against the unpadded fabric. Her eyes are wide and dilated.

Even though I am not the one who's been masturbating, my breathing matches hers, and I realize I cannot do this. I cannot stay away from her.

"Look what you do to me," I rasp. My free hand grips my erection through my pants, squeezing my cockhead almost to the point of pain.

Emma's eyes drop and widen even further. And then she licks her lips.

I release my hand from the door frame and take one step closer. Since Emma is my height, I can slide my cheek ever so gently against hers, just a whisper of a touch. "Your hand?" I ask.

She gives the barest of head shakes, and wisps of her gray hair tickle my nose. "A toy," she whispers, and my dick twitches in my hand. I inhale deeply through my nose, and I smell her floral shampoo, the tanginess of light sweat, and the barest musk of her arousal.

Someone opens the door downstairs, and voices filter in to pop our bubble. I step back, and our gazes lock.

"Bring it with you this weekend. Let's go away together."

Emma blinks, and the voices rise as they move past the stairwell and into the ground-floor hallway. "Where?"

"I have a house in the country."

She closes her eyes briefly and takes a deep breath. When she opens them, I get the barest of smiles—slightly nervous but mostly relieved. "Yes, okay."

The relief echoes through my body, tamping down the overwhelming lust. "I'll message you the details."

"Okay," Emma repeats.

I step back again and turn to walk away.

"Santo?" Emma calls before I get too far.

I half-turn to look back at her.

"Oliver's going to bark again."

"Yes, yes he is," I agree.

33

Emma

"So let me get this straight," Jade says, and I brace myself. It's the day after Santo's proposal, and I've just gotten home from classes, and we're video chatting. Tessa puts a hand over her mouth to preemptively stop a giggle, and Sara coughs. "The man who gave you the best orgasm of your life wants to take you away for a weekend so he can bang your brains out because it's too risky to bang here in the city?"

"Um, yes, well, I don't know if that was the best orgasm of my life—"

"*That's* what you want to argue about?"

Tessa snickers. She's in Paris visiting Luc this week, and I'm very glad that she has her earbuds in because they are living with Luc's elderly grandmother.

"Don't you think there's some recency bias here? Like surely back when Bruce—"

"No, no. I remember many nights where you were, frankly, agog at my bedroom shenanigans. Believe me when I tell you that there's no recency bias going on."

"Recency bias?" Sara asks.

"Fresh memories are more important than old ones in your brain, so you focus on them," Jade explains. "And also, he has a house somewhere?"

"Yes, in Castel Gandolfo. He texted me the address so I could send it to y'all. And since it'll be the end of the term, I miraculously don't have any homework."

"Right, because homework is a good reason not to have a weekend bang-fest."

"I have to keep my grades up! And I have to decide my concentration soon and then think about internships and—"

"You can do all of that while still having a weekend of amazing sex, I promise you."

"I *know*," I say, exasperated with Jade. "That's why I'm going to go."

"Hey, y'all?" Sara's voice interrupts us. "Has anyone Googled Santo?"

"No, why?" Jade's voice is sharp and concerned. "Are there, like, articles about how he's a serial killer who is so good he's left no evidence behind, and no one can get him convicted?"

"How would they know he's a serial killer if there's no evidence?" Tessa points out.

"There's circumstantial evidence, but not concrete evidence," Jade says. She loves true crime podcasts and has a weird fascination with unsolved murders. I know she's teasing, and I can hear the clacking of her keyboard as she Googles in her home office. I'm cooking dinner, so I let them do the searching for me. "Just enough for the Italian FBI to know it's him but not enough proof to put him away for life."

"You're imaginative," Sara says with fondness.

There's a moment of quiet, and when I look back at my phone, Sara's on the screen, her eyes scanning the area right below the camera. She's in her house in Austin, daylight filtering in through the window next to her. Her daughter is back in school, and Sara and Chris have spent their time in the US to be close to Zoe.

The view switches to Jade. "What do you know about Santo outside of class, Emma?"

I think for a minute. "There's a bio on the school's website, which I've read. He's divorced twice. He used to be in the tech industry."

"What about his dad?" Jade prompts.

I bite my lip. Santo told me about his dad in confidence, and I don't think I should tell them about the affair. It's too private and unrelated—it was his father who had the affair, not Santo.

"Not much," I admit.

"Emma, pick up your phone and google Franco Offredi."

I do, swiping up to relegate Jade's face to a tiny portion of the screen. The search results show me a variety of pictures through time of a man that has the same nose as Santo, same sharp gaze and coloring. Santo's father is broader, and when I see pictures of the two of them together I can see that their build is quite different.

My friends and I are quiet as we read for a few minutes. There's a helpful article about the height of Franco's company, Offredi Importazioni Globali, or OIG. There was the Italian economic miracle in the late sixties, where post-war Italy experienced an economic boom—and OIG, which imported everything from televisions to railroad supplies, rode the wave, eventually diversifying and expanding to become one of the largest companies in Italy, and Franco one of the richest men.

When I read his estimated net worth, I can't help the "oh shit," that falls from my mouth.

"Oh, shit is right," Jade remarks. "Santo is rich."

"Just because his dad was rich doesn't mean he is," Tessa points out. "While generational wealth is a big thing, this article says upon his death, most of his wealth was in the business. And Santo's CV on the school's website doesn't mention the company at all."

We keep reading and digging, going down a rabbit hole, until I smell something burning.

"Oh shit," I say again. I rush to the stovetop, where my dinner is smoking. Flipping the burner off, I peer into the pan. I forgot to set a timer, and now my quinoa and chicken are burned. Damn it. The smoke detector hasn't gone off yet, thank god, so I rush to the window to fling it open and let in the nippy January air.

This is the problem with one-dish meals. If you screw it up, then you are back to square one.

"You okay there, Emma?" Tessa asks, sounding amused. She's a skilled cook and I'd bet she's never burnt a meal in her life.

"Fine," I grumble, inspecting the pan. I poke at it with my spatula. The bottom is burned, but it was supposed to be tonight's dinner and leftovers. I think the top is salvageable, so I might get one plate out of it.

"Castel Gandolfo looks beautiful," Sara says wistfully.

That perks me up. "I know, I Googled it." It's a cute town on a lake surrounded by rolling hills. January isn't the best time to visit, but it's where many city folks—including, back in the day, the pope—spent their summers to get away from the stifling heat in the city. It's only an hour or so away.

"It'll be your own eat, pray, love journey," Tessa quips. "Without the praying."

Jade moans and pulls a When-Harry-Met-Sally-in-the-diner moment, her voice breathy and teasing. *"Oh, god."*

We laugh. "Okay, blasphemer. How about eat, sleep, love?"

I rub my forehead. "Not going to lie, sleep sounds so good right now."

After the conversation with Santo last night, I had a hard time focusing on my classwork. All last week, I gave myself more orgasms than I ever had in my life. I even pulled out my toy as soon as I got home today, but it only made me sad because I didn't even know if Santo was around and Oliver wasn't home to bark at me, either.

"I say go for it," Jade announces.

"Color me surprised," Tessa deadpans.

"What about his job? Her reputation at school?" Normally, I'm the one who's the pessimist, but Sara's always willing to take up the mantle for me.

They bicker back and forth for a bit—guess who says, "but sneaking around is so hot"?—until I interrupt them. "There is one other concern that I have."

"Aside from the secrecy and the risks?"

"Yeah." I fidget with the fringe on the throw blanket on the couch. "So, he's definitely given me my best orgasm ever. I doubt I can return the favor. What if when we have sex, it's not that great?"

"Babe," Jade begins. "You're my best friend. We just lived together for a month. I know you better than I know anyone else in my life—sorry, ladies."

Tessa smirks, and Sara waves it off.

Jade leans into the camera, pressing her palms together in supplication. "Do you think that I would release you unprepared into the world of fucking? Knowledge is power, and I've spent our whole friendship arming you with the biggest weapons in my arsenal: feel good about yourself, don't forget to laugh, ask for what you want, be open to experimenting, don't do anything you aren't comfortable with, tight and wet are compliments of the patriarchy, always get your orgasm first—"

"Okay, okay," I say, laughing and holding my hands up in defeat. "You're right. The sex will probably be the best I've ever had, too, and hopefully, it'll be good for him. I just wish you had, like, a secret weapon for me."

Jade peers off and to the right side of the camera, tapping

her chin. "Well, there is one thing you could do that would probably blow his mind. If he's up for it."

"What?" I lean in, curiosity getting the better of me. I know the things Jade likes—light bondage, hair pulling, spanking—but I don't really know what she has in mind.

Sara and Tessa don't seem to know either, and they've both leaned in further.

"It requires a bit of prep work, and the guy has to be pretty open-minded about it, but…"

———

"OH, MY GOD." I SAID IT ABOUT A MILLION TIMES ON OUR DRIVE to the countryside, and I'm saying it again from the terrace of Santo's villa. He's still calling it a house, but it's a villa—terra cotta tiles, earthy tones inside and outside, and a gorgeous view of the surrounding vineyards. Since we left right after class, it's dusk, and while the sun might still be above the horizon, it's sunk behind the hills that shadow the valleys of the landscape.

I should help—the car door slams shut from the other side of the house, and I know Santo is getting my bag for me, but I can't peel my eyes from the Cyprus trees and rolling plains. He's also getting Zola situated since we brought her for the weekend, so she doesn't have to be alone.

I take some pictures. I want to send them to my kids, but I don't know how to explain that I'm out of town on a romantic weekend with anyone, let alone my professor. If one of them was doing this with a professor, I would fly home to open a giant can of angry momma bear ass on them.

Hypocritical, maybe. But despite Santo's position at the school, I can't see what we're doing as wrong, at least not when I'm around him. My kids are still developing; they're still young enough to be learning hard lessons and making mistakes. I'm older and wiser (I like to think), and so is Santo. He's so responsible—for that matter, I usually am too—and a naive part of me thinks that this isn't a big deal.

Currently, that part in my head sounds like Jade, which is ironic because she's the least naive person I know.

I send the pictures to our group chat instead. Tessa immediately responds with a heart-eyes emoji. Sara's probably teaching back in Austin, but a few minutes later, Jade texts back.

JADE

Eat, sleep, BANG.

Are you ready to blow his mind?

I bite my lip. I haven't asked Santo about my plans yet, though I came prepared. And I've read about a dozen articles Jade sent me.

But we're not starting with that; at least, I hope not. If Santo is totally grossed out by the idea when I ask him on Sunday, then we can call it quits early and head back to the city.

And that will be that.

A throat clears behind me, and I turn to see Santo stepping out onto the terrace. He's got two glasses of sparkling wine, and he holds one out to me. "Prosecco," he tells me.

"Thank you," I say, taking the glass from him. "For this and for bringing me here. It's so beautiful."

He shrugs modestly. "It's better in the summer. More lush and vibrant, though I enjoy the quiet of the winter here." He holds his flute up to me. "Saluti."

"Saluti," I echo and gently touch my glass to his.

The wine is bubbly and crisp, tickling my nose as I sip. "How long have you owned this place?"

"Oh, let me see…eighteen—no, nineteen years now. My father suggested I buy a place away from the city, and I liked the idea. I didn't use it much until I started teaching. Just the summer holiday, usually, but I always brought work with me."

The summer holiday, I've learned, is when many Europeans take the month of August off. When I was in Madrid with Jade, we spent a week in Majorca, though it was crowded and hot, and Jade often had to speak with her American counterparts back in the States who did not have the month of August off.

"Well, no work this weekend, right?"

"No, all fun." Santo snakes his arm around my waist and pulls me closer to him. "All…pleasure." He whispered the last word against my cheek.

I wrap my free arm around his neck as his mouth softens and travels down the side of my face to my neck. A gasp escapes my lips as he plants an open-mouth kiss on my pulse point.

There's a scrape of teeth, and then he sucks, and I feel it all the way down to my toes, which curl in my flats. I squeeze my thighs together, and the seam of my jeans is my new favorite thing.

Santo pulls back, keeping his arm around my waist. All I can do is pant.

Fuck recency bias. I'm pretty confident I've never felt like this before.

Santo's eyes are dark, pupils dilated, and the brown of his irises is lost in the dimming light. The sky is deepening to shades of blue, shadows emerging in the harsh light that shines on us from inside.

Santo doesn't take his eyes off me as he lifts the wine to his lips and swallows the rest of it. He places the empty glass on an old barrel that doubles as a table.

"Emma," he rasps. "Do you want your wine?"

I blink and stare at my wine glass like I've never seen it

before. Liquid courage, but I don't know that I need it. "No,"
I tell him.

Santo sets the wine glass down next to his and tangles his
hand with mine, tugging me toward the indoors.

34

Santo

With Emma's huge, sweet eyes looking up at me, I recognize that I'm making a mistake already. This weekend will be unlike any other I've ever had, not the rush of young love and hectic schedules or the slow consideration of dating a woman with a child or the immediacy of a one-night stand, but a seduction. I can see it in Emma's face, how ripe and eager she is for it as I shift her long gray hair over her shoulder and trace a finger down the edge of her blouse.

She already drives me wild, and this possessiveness that surges through me when I look at her makes me wonder how no one else has seen it.

I bend my head and kiss her clavicle, then scrape my teeth along it. It's one of the few places she isn't all lush and soft curves, and the contrast of it against the curve of her hip in my hand makes me want to kiss every inch of her, discover where she's soft and those hidden places where she isn't.

Stomach. The soft crook where her arm meets her torso. The fold where ass meets thigh.

Elbows. Knuckles. Ankles.

"Santo," she whispers, a hitch in her voice. I remember myself and ease away, lightly running kisses over where I've left teeth marks.

"Shit, I'm sorry—"

Emma grabs my head, her fingers twining through my hair, and lowers my head back down. "I liked it," she pants.

Instead of biting again, I smooth the skin with my lips, and in response, Emma's hips thrust against mine. I snake one hand down to her ass, savoring the roughness of the jeans against my palm until I can cup one cheek. She's tense, her body clenched and pulsing against nothing.

I can give her something to press against.

Reaching further, I slide my fingers between her legs from behind. The angle is challenging, and she has to rise to her tiptoes, but it's worth it when I feel the heat of her core through the thick material, her thighs squeezing together and her body instinctively rubbing against my hand.

I bend down to chest level, and I nuzzle the valley between her breasts while Emma grinds. She's still gripping my hair, not guiding me but grounding her. My erection, mostly ignored, strains against my pants.

Emma gives such a hard thrust we both wobble, and she lands back on her heels with a jerk. "Santo," she pants. "Bed."

I straighten and tug her hand, leading her back to the master bedroom. Earlier, I'd turned on the lamps, which cast a soft, warm light around the room. I shed my jacket and shoes, going for efficiency instead of sensuality. Emma seems to agree because I've barely gotten a shoe off before her top is flying over her head and landing on her suitcase in a heap.

Emma's naked first and strips the bedding back before crawling in. The sight of her on her hands and knees ensures that if I wasn't hard already, I would be. I tuck my thumbs in the waistband of my black briefs and slip them off, tossing them somewhere in the same direction as the rest of my clothes.

Placing a knee on the bed, I grab one of Emma's ankles and tug it, spreading her legs open for me. Ever since she came on my mouth ages ago, I've been wanting to do it again. Knowing that I've pleasured her better than any other man gives me a deep sense of satisfaction.

"Santo, can you please just fuck me."

I stop staring at her cunt and meet her eyes. "Are you going to be able to come on my cock?"

Her eyelids flutter, and her ankle tugs my hand as she tries to squeeze her thighs together. I don't think she even knows she's doing it.

"Probably not," she admits. "But I really need you." It ends on a whine. "I've been thinking about that ever since you suggested we go away together." Her cheeks, already flushed a pretty pink, darken. "Well, that's not true. It's been a lot longer than that."

I stretch up and kiss her. "I've been thinking about licking that pretty figa ever since the last time you came on my tongue. No, since the very first time I tasted you. Ergo," I say, and she laughs. "I get my wish first."

"If we're going all the way back," she starts, "then— ughm."

I lick straight up her pussy, and her head rolls back, words forgotten. I slide my tongue up and down, using my hands on her thighs to spread her apart and worship her. This time, it doesn't take as long for her to be squirming and panting, restlessly kicking at the sheets. I take the bud of her clit into my mouth and suck. I'm rewarded with her thighs clenching around my head, and within a few minutes, she's crying out my name, pulsing against my tongue and I'm licking up all of her sweet juices.

When she goes limp, I pull back with one soft kiss on her thigh. "Still want to fuck, piccola?" I ask.

"Oh god, yes," she says without hesitation, and I rise and pad over to my luggage, digging out condoms and lube. I toss the closed bottle of the latter on the bed and rip open the former, rolling it down my shaft.

Emma's legs fall open again as I kneel between them. I hook one arm under her knee, spreading her open and using the other hand to guide myself in. She's still slick from her orgasm, and I pump slowly, in and then out a bit and in a little bit more until I bottom out.

Looking up, Emma's cheeks and chest are all flushed a brilliant soft pink. Her rosebud of a mouth is slightly parted, and those beautiful eyes watch me.

I lean down, pressing my hand into the mattress above her shoulder, and kiss her. I match the strokes of my cock inside of her with my tongue until I have to back away to breathe. Through barely open eyes, I watch Emma; her eyelids are closed in pleasure. She said she didn't think she could come on my cock, and I had hoped to switch up to some way that we could stimulate her clit too, but the urge at the base of my spine is telling me there's no time. I'll have to spend the rest of the weekend figuring out how to do that because right now, an enraged bull couldn't stop me from finishing.

I thrust harder, knocking a cry out of Emma. One of her hands grips my forearm where I'm braced against the bed, the other slides over my ribs. After a few more moments of her mewing, I take one last thrust deep inside of her, and shudder out my orgasm.

35

Emma

Santo collapses next to me. We're both breathing hard, my body still fluttering and wonderfully satiated, even though I didn't orgasm with the penetration.

I glance over at Santo. His hair is disheveled, and he has two spots of color on his cheeks that I've never seen before. Despite the chill in the air, we broke a sweat, and the combination of that and the scents of our arousal and clean sheets is heady.

Santo turns his head to look at me, and slowly, both our smiles bloom. He rolls toward me, palm slipping over the curve of my belly to settle on my hip. "Would you like to clean up first?"

I groan and theatrically drag myself out of bed, leaving Santo behind chuckling. I flip the light on in the bathroom and glance back. The bedroom is softly lit, so the light from the bathroom casts a bright spotlight on the bed, which feels poignant.

At the head of the bed in the shadows, I can barely make out Santo's eyes on my body. Feeling saucy—a new feeling!

When was the last time I was saucy?—I jut out a hip before closing the door.

When we switch places, I pull the sheet up to my armpits and prop myself up on the headboard and look around.

His villa is beyond what I'd imagined. It's somehow rustic and classy, ironically reminding me of the refurbished items we sold at Second Chances. I know nothing about real estate in Italy, but this must be an expensive place. It's also huge. The common areas are large and vaulted, and Santo told me there are four bedrooms.

And I know Santo comes from money. I pull the covers up further. It's early, and we haven't eaten yet, so I doubt we are going to sleep, but the bed is comfortable, and I am loath to leave this room.

Santo must feel the same because he slides back into bed after he's done in the restroom.

"I Googled you," I blurt.

Santo freezes for a moment and then relaxes next to me. "You Googled me?" he echoes.

"Yeah. Sorry, I felt weird not telling you I know about your family business now and the, um…"

"Money?" he guesses.

"Yeah." I shift to face him. "You told me about your dad's affair."

Santo sighs. "Yes. But I think this conversation requires a drink. Would you like more Prosecco?"

Oooh, post-sex bubbly. "Yes, please."

Santo walks out of the room buck naked and returns a minute or so later with two refilled glasses of wine. He settles back into bed, and we clink glasses. The wine is light and crisp and very good after a round of hot sex.

"Is Prosecco your favorite?" Santo asks. "It occurs to me I keep bringing you more and you may not like it so much. Do you have a wine you like better?"

I shake my head. "You're right. Prosecco is my favorite. I

mean, out of what I've tried, I guess, which isn't much." Our shoulders are lightly brushing, almost tickling me, so I lean against Santo a bit, pressing our upper arms firmly together. "My ex-in-laws once bought us a nice bottle of champagne. It had a yellow label, but I forget the brand, like Vu-something-something—"

"Veuve Clicquot."

"Yes, that one!" I sound out the name, and he repeats it for me until I can pronounce it correctly.

"The widow," he adds.

"What?"

"That's what veuve means. Widow Clicquot. A woman founded the house."

"Really? When?" I have no idea how long it would take to grow a champagne empire that's so recognizable.

"Oh," Santo thinks. "Seventeen seventies, maybe? You should look her up. She was groundbreaking."

Jesus. My country, if it was even a country yet, was a baby when that wine was made. "I will," I promise. "Anyway, I didn't love it, so I stayed away from bubbly for a while. But my friends and I often met at a wine bar, and I tried a few different things before I had my first glass of Prosecco, and I love it. So no, I won't turn a glass down."

Our legs are touching slightly, too, and I shift, and my foot rubs against his. He nudges it, and somehow, my leg ends up over his, my thighs slightly spread and my heel under his calf.

"Do you not want to talk about your dad?" I bring the conversation back.

"It's fine," Santo says. "Do you remember in the first term you told me you were trying to prove to yourself and your ex that you could do it without him?"

I nod.

"That's all my father desired from me. He wanted me to have nothing to do with his business, so he was constantly pushing me away from it. At the time, all *I* wanted was to be spending time with him, and all he did was work. Looking back, I see my father was perhaps jealous that I had achieved so much. Even my successes were not mine because everyone knew who I was, and his name carried a lot of weight. So, you Googling me and learning about my past is not troublesome. I'm surprised you didn't already know, actually."

"Your bio at the school has no mention of it."

"Ah, yes. Well, perhaps I wrote it while in the mood to snub my father." He's quiet for a moment before he switches the glass to his far hand and lifts the near one, wrapping it around my shoulders.

"What about your parents?" Santo asks.

I tell him about my mom, who died when I was a newlywed, and my dad, who passed away a few years ago. He'd remarried and was living in Houston, and we had grown distant. I ask about Santo's mom—I know she died years ago, thanks to my internet sleuthing—and am told a sad story of a woman scorned who never recovered.

We should discuss something lighter. There are a few sips of Prosecco left in my glass, but I'm saving it so we don't feel the need to get up yet. "Where's Zola?" I haven't seen the cat at all since Santo let her loose in the house.

"She has her own room."

"Like the loft back in the city?" I tease.

"Even nicer," he admits. "She's a little spoiled here."

"*Here?*" I tilt my head to look at Santo. "She's a little spoiled in the city. She must be a queen here." Santo chuckles. His empty wine glass is on the bedside table, and his free hand comes under the sheet and strokes the inside of my thigh, not so high that he's going to accidentally touch between my legs, but enough to give me shivers.

And then my stomach rumbles. Santo chuckles and my body bounces. I finally toss back the last of the wine as Santo slips out of bed.

"I got you something," he says, surprising me.

"You did?"

I untangle myself from the sheets while Santo opens a wardrobe and pulls out an occupied hanger. On it is a long bathrobe—light gray with a barely-there geometric pattern on the lapels. There are matching slippers, too, and when I reach out and touch the material, it's so fine and soft it feels like silk.

"It's cashmere," Santo says, "so you'll have to be careful washing it or maybe have a cleaner take care of it. But I thought perhaps if I have one weekend with you, I want you to be warm and comfortable and as close to naked as possible."

He helps me slip it on and tie the belt around my waist. I don't think I've owned anything so luxurious.

"Warmer, yes?"

"Yes," I agree.

"No more catching pneumonia. Not on my watch."

I laugh as Santo dresses himself in pants and a T-shirt. "I still can't believe how sick I was after that weekend in Zurich. Shonda teases me about the weather all the time, says this is *mild.*"

In the kitchen, we put together an antipasto platter and pour more wine. At the table, we eat, talking and enjoying each other's company. First, I'm ravenous, and the salty olives and smoked almonds are hitting the spot. Santo feeds me his favorite salami, which he calls spianata romana. When we finish ravaging the platter, Santo's hand slides under the table and onto my cashmere-covered leg.

We're talking about Abelie's and my children's teenage years, and swapping horror stories about boundaries being pushed, so at first Santo's hand is just a simple gesture of affection. Then it slides down and finds the edges of the robe and comes to rest on my bare thigh, his thumb idly stroking while telling me about Abelie sneaking cigarettes into his house on a visit.

It's distracting, though, and soon I squirm. "Santo." My voice has a note of whining to it. I'm getting slick with arousal and am very aware that I have no underwear on. "I don't want to get the cashmere dirty."

He leans in, a wicked grin on his face. "Why don't we go get my face dirty instead?"

36

Emma

I'M IN POSITION AND SURPRISINGLY NERVOUS FOR SOMEONE WHO'S not on the receiving end. Santo is lying on the bed, a delicious buffet of olive skin and sparse brown hair. His hands are behind his head, his eyes watching me softly.

I'm kneeling between his legs, the pointer finger of my right hand slicked up with lube. I was feeling pretty good about it up to this moment.

Yesterday had been exactly what I had dreamed it would be—an eat, sleep, bang-fest with Santo all day. We got out of bed to eat. In the morning, I had a cup of coffee, and he joined me with a plate of pastries. Lunch, we enjoyed al fresco on the balcony, clad in only our underwear with my robe and blankets and a view. For dinner, Santo cooked while I sat at the counter, drinking wine and being hand-fed prosciutto and fresh bread, then a simple pasta dish and in-season blood oranges for dessert.

Between meals, we dozed and talked and had sex, though it felt uneven. We only had penetrative sex a few times, and sometimes Santo didn't orgasm, but he didn't seem to mind.

Instead, he used his mouth and his hands frequently, and I'd lost count of how many times I'd come.

This morning, when I told Santo I wanted to play with his prostate, he looked thoughtful and mused that he'd never done it before. When I explained the prep work, he gently told me he was familiar with how anal sex works, though that was something I wasn't going to think too hard about.

After Jade's explanation, I read about fifteen articles on the topic—articles that got passed around our group chat because I wasn't the only one interested in this kind of play, apparently.

Santo drops a hand to his chest, and I turn my attention back to the task at hand, so to speak. I read some men can come hands free and some can't, so I get into position over his hips, one elbow at his side holding most of my weight. It's pretty unsexy until I reach down and press a kiss to the tendon that runs from Santo's thigh to his groin, and he inhales sharply. He's hard and has been since he laid down on the bed and watched me prepare, although I think that was less about the anticipation of the act and more about seeing me doing, well, *anything* while naked.

I run my lips up and down his shaft. Without saliva or lube or pre-come, his skin beneath mine is so soft. I press light, closed-mouth kisses on the vein that runs along the underside of his cock and on the rim of the crown, avoiding the bead of moisture coming out.

I do this for as long as I can until Santo gives a hoarse "Emma…" and I pop the head into my mouth. Santo is uncut, so I have the foreskin to play with too, and I swallow and lick and suck until Santo vibrates with tension.

Then I rest my hand on his ass cheek, skimming his balls with my fingers. My finger moves down until the tip, slipped with lube, rests against his hole, and Santo breathes deeply and relaxes under me.

I push in gently, pumping a bit to make sure he's properly slicked up. At the second knuckle, I stop, focusing my attention back on his cock, which has gone soft. I use my mouth and my free hand to tease him again, taking him as deep as I can and then jacking him off. When he's nice and hard again, I crook that finger inside him, and Santo's whole body jerks.

"Fuck." He raises his head to look down at me, eyes wide. "Do that again. Please, Emma."

All the instructions said that the prostate would be spongy, and they were right. It's more noticeable than I thought it would be. I rub small circles against it, and Santo's head falls back again, his hands gripping the sheets on either side of him. One knee comes up, giving me more access, and I suckle on his cockhead while continuing that slow, steady pressure on his prostate, over and over again. Time flies by with Santo groaning and panting and quivering, and I've never felt so sexy in my life. He can't even see me, and I feel like a goddess.

"Oh fuck, oh fuck," Santo chants. "I'm…god, Emma!"

His whole body curves up, those gorgeous muscles honed from soccer games flexing and twisting. Inside, his prostate hardens, and I slip my mouth off his cock and focus on stroking him with my hands, long and hard from both sides.

Santo lets out a string of curse words, some English, some Italian, and power courses through me as he comes. This is exactly what I wanted, this feeling like I've returned the favor, that Santo is just as overwhelmed by me in bed as I am by him.

Santo finishes ejaculating, but his head is still thrown back, eyes screwed shut in pleasure, and his hips give these small thrusts, almost fucking back against my finger until a switch flips, and Santo falls back against the bed. "Okay, okay." He's laughing and shuddering against the overstimulation, so I stop all movements and wait.

Santo rubs his face with his hands. "Jesus Cristo, è stato

fantastico," he says. "Fuck." He drops his hands to his chest. "Come here, piccola."

I carefully ease my finger out, and then dart to the bathroom and wash my hands before returning to Santo. His fingers thread through my hair, tugging me down to a hard, demanding kiss. It's hot and wet and makes me forget everything I was doing, smoothing away any lingering doubts I had.

When we part, I'm lying on my side, curled up next to him. Santo leans his forehead against mine. "That was amazing," he says.

I can't help the giant smile that comes over my face, and Santo laughs and presses a kiss to my cheek. Then he flops back down again, still panting.

I lay down, too, and a few minutes later, Santo rolls out of bed to go clean up. When he returns to the room, Santo stretches out on the sheets. He gestures me over, and I return to the same position, my head at the spot where his chest meets his shoulder.

Santo strokes my hair lazily, and I trace my fingers over his nipple before following the hair to the center of his chest.

"Time for a nap?" I ask, and he hums.

Despite my suggestion, I don't close my eyes, and instead just listen to his heartbeat and his breathing. He must be doing the same, though, because a few minutes later he speaks.

"What do you think about when I eat your figa?"

My hand stills before I start it up again. I consider being vague—masturbating or sex or something—but then Santo was already so open-minded with me, willing to take my finger up his ass, and if you can't be honest with a man after that, when can you?

"I mostly think about women masturbating." Santo's fingers in my hair keep up their steady rhythm, so I continue, telling him things I've never told anyone else. "Sometimes I watch porn, and I picture my favorite videos. And I enjoy watching women get off. Um, on a Sybian, specifically." I clear my throat. The pommel-like sex toy is huge and powerful and also quite expensive. I've never even dreamed of owning one. "I kind of have a thing for women on Sybians."

My head bounces once as Santo huffs a laugh. "What a coincidence. I think I could very well have a thing for you on a Sybian."

I laugh too.

"Have you ever been with anyone who wasn't a man?" Santo asks.

"No. I've only ever been with Bruce, and now you. I've had crushes, I suppose. I don't know if I would want to. But it's fun to think about."

His arm around me squeezes, and he changes the topic. "How did you decide you wanted to try this prostate play?"

I tell him about my phone call with my friends and how Jade suggested this. "So, technically, I think you can thank her."

"No," he says softly. "She may have given you the idea but you were the one who was brave enough to ask me." He tilts my chin up and gives me a soft kiss. "Thank you for a weekend I'll never forget."

37

Emma

"AND HOW WAS IT?" JADE ASKS FROM THE SCREEN OF MY LAPTOP. It's Sunday night, and Santo and I are back in our separate apartments. After unpacking my stuff, starting a load of laundry, and ordering take out, I messaged my friends to let them know I was home, and immediately they wanted to debrief. "Did you do the thing?"

I remember the feel of Santo's body clenching around mine and the look of sheer, excruciating pleasure when he came, and I can't help the huge smile that grows.

"Damn," Jade says, laughing. "That good, huh?"

I put my face in my hands, laughing too. "It was so good. Like, the perfect time away. I don't think I'd ever had that many orgasms in a weekend." It wasn't just the orgasms, of course, but it's hard to explain the way Santo looked at me when he was ready for another round, or how he brought food in bed when I was too sexed-out to get up, or how when we showered together mid-afternoon yesterday, in the bright lights of the bathroom, I hadn't felt self-conscious at all. Santo had put his hands all over me by that point, and he knew

227

every stretch mark and freckle. Every place of my body that I didn't like, he'd seen. And he'd still wanted me right up until we kissed goodbye.

"Good job, Santo," Tessa cheers from her apartment in Portugal.

"Is there going to be a repeat performance?" Sara asks. She's back home in Austin with Chris, but they'll be flying back to Europe soon. Next weekend we're going to Malta together to escape the winter weather.

"No," I say, and I'm surprised how sad I sound.

"Do you want more?" Jade asks, and my friends all peer at me through their screens.

Santo and I have chemistry in bed—amazing chemistry. Unexpected chemistry. Thinking back on the weekend, I realize that there was something more important at play here, too; a part of me had always worried that the best of my life had passed. I am a forty-two-year-old divorcee and mother of three. I am bigger than all my friends, less worldly, less comfortable in my body.

And yet, instead of comparing myself to slim, elegant European women, I am having the best sex of my life.

If I can have the best sex of my life now, why can't I have the love of my life?

Okay, back up. I have a lot of feelings about Santo, but love isn't one of them. I respect him a lot. He is a great professor who clearly cares about his students and their education. As an ex-stepfather to Bell, he goes above and beyond what many men do when they get divorced. I know some dads who aren't as close to their own kids as Santo is to Bell.

Most importantly, I've learned so much about myself over the time that I've known him. I am grateful for that. I like him, on top of being wildly attracted to him.

I rub my forehead, and my friends wait while I gather my thoughts. What do I want?

Next door, Oliver barks. I straighten and listen, my heart-beat racing already. What is Oliver barking at?

"Emma?" Sara's voice calls my attention back to the screen. But I have to know what Oliver's barking at.

"I have to go. Love you!" I shut the lid of my laptop, cutting my friends' protests off, and rush to the door. I skid into the hallway just as Santo's door opens and he lurches out.

We stand in the hallway, breathing hard and staring at each other.

"Were you...?" Santo runs a hand through his hair. He's dressed in a T-shirt and long pants, his glasses slightly crooked and the short, black hairs on his shirt tell me he was cuddling with Zola.

"No. Were you?"

He shakes his head. Oliver lets out one final bark and then the hallway goes quiet. Santo's gaze remains on mine for a few beats. "Come here," he rasps out.

I shut my door and walk to him. When I get in range, he reaches for me, and with his fingers tangled in my hair and his body walking mine into his apartment, Santo kisses me.

Half an hour later, Santo and I are a sweaty mess on his bed, catching our breath. Weirdly, Oliver didn't bark at us at all. "I had a theory, but I think we just disproved it," I say, tucking the sheet under my arms and propping myself up on my elbow to face Santo. He glances at me before rolling to his side, too, mirroring me.

"What was your theory?"

"Oliver is an agent of the Catholic Church, and he's working to curb masturbation and premarital sex."

Santo falls onto his back, laughing. His grin is wide as he gestures to the wall. "But he didn't bark."

"Exactly. Theory disproved. Do *you* have a theory about why he barks at us?"

Santo gets back into position, eyes twinkling with laughter. "I think he is trying to protect us. We're alone, and there are sounds of distress. Eva needs to be alerted."

"Like a support animal, but instead of helping her open doors or guiding her, he's being a concerned neighbor."

Santo looks at the wall above us and rubs his chin. "What do you think would happen if we masturbated right now?"

We share a look and then roll onto our backs. Santo kicks off the sheet and takes his soft cock in his hand. I spread my legs and touch myself, stroking my clit. I'm still a little slick from the lube we used, so I close my eyes and replay the sex we just had–me on my back, legs wrapped around Santo's hips as he stands beside the bed, thrusting into me. He had his thumb on my clit too, and I came twice before we finished. Which is why I'm feeling a little sore now, my clit irritated from a weekend full of stimulation.

I hear a rustle and feel a small dip. When I open my eyes, Santo is sitting up and watching me. When his eyes travel back up to look at my face, we both grin.

"No barking," he says, and I stop touching myself. Santo raises an eyebrow. "No more?"

"No more," I agree. "Not tonight, anyway."

Santo falls back next to me. "What do you want to do beyond that?" he asks, resting his head on the pillow.

"I had a really great weekend with you," I confess, looking into his eyes. "Not just the sex. I had fun."

"So did I. I was just sitting with Zola, thinking about how I didn't want it to be over. But I haven't had a relationship in a long time. Not since Bell's mother."

"And I've only just started…well. I guess we're not really dating."

Santo sighs. "Do you want to get married again someday?"

I scoff. "I don't even know where I'm going to be in two months, let alone what I'll be doing after the program is over."

"True. But still, I think we should keep this quiet. I'm sorry."

"No, it's okay. I get it. And maybe I can change to another professor for the term." I am supposed to be in Santo's Technology and Innovation Management class starting tomorrow.

"I can drop the course, tell the director I've had something come up, and he can find someone else to teach it."

I press a kiss to Santo's shoulder. Santo is the best professor the school has. He cares about his students, and I know that this is important to him. "It should be me."

Absent-mindedly, Santo strokes my arm and doesn't argue. A few minutes later, Zola jumps up onto the bed and curls up behind my legs. She didn't sleep with us over the weekend, so this is new. I'm warm and sleepy and sexually exhausted. For the third night in a row, I fall asleep in Santo's arms.

38

Santo

IT TAKES A FEW DAYS, BUT EMMA GETS HER SCHEDULE CHANGED, and for the first time, I don't have her in my lectures, but we are spending more time than ever together. Ironically, I get more work done, making more progress on my book while I stay up late waiting for Emma to finish studying and come over. Sometimes, I message asking if she's had dinner yet, and when she suggests ordering dinner, I cook for her instead.

For the first time since that night months ago when I met Emma, I feel like I can be myself around her. I enjoy making her laugh and blush and then chasing that blush across her skin with my lips.

Zola has even started waiting for Emma by the door. She still snoozes on my chest in the evenings, but curling up with us in bed at night is new.

Bell comes over for dinner one night with Emma and me. Emma chooses her concentration for the next phase of the program—luxury business management. I feel good enough to start playing football again. Everything is going well, domestic, even.

Emma goes to London with her friends for the weekend near the end of the fourth term. She's taken to studying at my place, and with her gone, it feels empty when I'm home. I call Vincente to see if he wants to come over and watch a match.

It's Roma versus Lazio, and while Vincente doesn't play like I do, he follows Roma closely. We cheer and shout at the TV, and Zola hides up in the loft. Roma wins, of course, and after finishing his beer, Vincente puts his jacket on and heads for the door.

He stops as he's passing the kitchen island, though, and peers at something on the counter.

My heart races when I realize what he's looking at. Emma left some of her work on my counter. This morning, I'd stacked it up to the side, but the spiral notebooks are open to her wide and messy handwriting.

Vincente looks at me, and his hands slow as he zips his jacket. "What is this?"

I don't want to lie to Vincente any more than I have to, but in this, I'm caught. I rub my hand over my beard. "Emma left those behind and I am returning them to her."

"Left them behind where?"

"Vincente."

He crosses his arms. "I noticed she's not in any of your courses this term. Does that make you feel better about it?"

"I don't–"

"Don't lie to me again," he says, voice cutting. "Actually, I'll make it easier for you not to lie to me right now." Vincente turns and walks out my door.

When Emma gets home, I tell her about the incident.

"Are you worried? Should we do something?"

I run my hand through my hair. "Technically, the university doesn't have rules on relations. Italy doesn't have Title IX like the US does, and all we have is a vague ethics policy. I should have said something, probably." Ever since Vincente left, this has been gnawing at me, and it probably should have been gnawing at me sooner than that. I've just been too damn happy.

"Santo," Emma says gently. "I didn't expect to be here, and neither did you. None of this was expected, and I haven't, at any point, felt like you abused your position."

We let it go, and another week goes by. I barely see Vincente, but this isn't the first time he's been mad at me, so I just hope that it'll blow over soon. Being with Emma makes it easy to think about other things.

So, when Director Greco calls me into his office, I think it's going to be a conversation about my book or an update on fundraising.

Instead, when I enter his office, there's a woman from our HR department in attendance, and Greco tells me to have a seat. He leans in, steepling his fingers.

"Santo, your contract with the university is terminated, effective immediately."

39

Emma

I'VE BEEN CALLED TO THE PRINCIPAL'S OFFICE. OR AT LEAST, that's what it feels like. I got an email during my third class telling me to see Director Greco immediately after class. Of course, that means I spend the rest of my Digital Strategy class distracted, wondering what I could be meeting with the director for.

Is this about my concentration selection? I'd chosen the Luxury Business Management route. I don't know much about luxury brands when it comes to clothes or jewelry, but even back when I'd been working with Bruce, I'd known in my gut that we could drive a higher market price and that product scarcity would work for us. It was something that, looking back, I'd always been proud of understanding without having the knowledge or training. I knew that Second Chances couldn't compete with Ikea and Target, so that wasn't our goal. When Bruce had wanted to set our prices low, I'd pushed back. And that friction had paid off in the long run.

With that decided, I had to apply for internships and

choose my coursework for my concentration. My internship could be anywhere—the school had relationships with a variety of companies all over Europe and Asia—and the classes would be taught online. Santo and I had talked about what we would do next, but it was hard to figure it out before I knew where I was going. If I stayed nearby, we might start dating for real—publicly. But if it was far away…

Class ends, and I realize I will have to ask some of my classmates for notes on our homework since I haven't been paying attention. I pack my things and make my way to the administrative hall. My nerves are unsettled, and something doesn't feel right, even though I don't know what it is.

Director Greco's receptionist ushers me into his office. There is a woman I don't recognize already at one of the chairs opposite Greco, and she smiles at me while the director gestures to the empty seat. The door clicks shut behind me, and I try not to take it ominously.

Greco folds his hands on the desk and gives me a small smile. "Ms. Chance, good to see you again."

"Thank you." I've only met him a few times over the months, and I kind of doubt that he recognizes me.

"I had a conversation with Valerius Botanicals this morning. They've extended an offer for you as an intern."

The unease vanishes, and I grin. Valerius is my first choice, an Italian company with an internship that focused on sourcing and purchasing out of their London office. "Really?" I grip the arms of the chair in an effort to control my excitement. "Oh, that's amazing."

"Yes." The faint smile is still there but twists a bit. More… melancholy? Why? This is great news.

"However, we have some concerns about your grades over the business fundamentals terms, specifically in relation to your coursework done under the purview of Professor Offredi."

The smile slides off my face. "What?"

Greco's smile is gone, too. "We have reason to believe that there was a bias in reporting, and to be fair to all students, we are going to require some retesting."

"Retesting?"

"Yes, we will have an additional examination period for you to determine that your coursework was truely up to our standards before we move forward with the internship. Unfortunately, with time constraints and the ending of the fourth term approaching, this won't be possible until the first week of March."

"Wait, wait." My brain is catching up. "Santo can clea–"

Greco stops me. *"Professor Offredi"*—the rebuke for using his first name is clear—"is no longer involved with the university."

My mouth hangs open. Santo was fired? Or did he quit? Again, Greco cuts me off before I can ask any of these questions.

"Let's focus on your education, Ms. Chance. I have a schedule here for the administration of your test and the professors who will proctor them."

He hands me a sheet of paper with dates and times printed next to the names of three classes. The dates stare up at me, and something clicks in my mind. "When does my internship start?" My voice is weak, and the paper trembles a little when I pick it up.

"Due to the circumstances, I recommended to Valerius that they look for an alternative. Their internship starts immediately following the finals for term four, and your credits will be held until your retesting."

My internship is gone. "What happens if I score lower on my tests than I did during the term?" There have been months and nearly a dozen courses between my first class and now. I'm not a top student as it is. It's very likely I don't remember as much as I need to from these courses.

"We just need you to pass. You'll have a week between the

end of your fourth term and the testing, so you can review the course materials."

"But…I applied to internships based on the original grades. Valerius made an offer based on those scores."

"Yes. We have full confidence that if your scores are still passing, we will be able to find a new internship opportunity for you." Greco gives me a long look. "Is there anything else, Ms. Chance?"

Is there anything else? There's so much I don't know where to start, and I just shake my head. Numb, I shuffle out of the office escorted by the woman. We walk down the hallway in silence, and my mind replays the meeting over and over again. Did that just happen? Am I going to lose everything I came to Rome to get?

We turn a corner, and a tug on my elbow stops me. I look down at the woman next to me who releases my elbow and pulls out a business card. "Go home and try to breathe, yes? If you need more options, or if there is something I can do to help, call me."

I take the card, and she turns around, the sound of her heels clicking away behind me. I flip the card over. It has her name, Nicole Palerma, and beneath that, Dipartimento Risorse Umane/Human Resources.

40

Santo

IT'S ON MY FIFTY-SEVENTH TRIP BACK AND FORTH IN THE HALLWAY that Emma finally arrives home. She's paler than usual, her eyes unfocused, and her hand grips the stairwell railing tightly as she trudges up the stairs.

She stops when she sees me, and my heart stutters.

"Emma..." I don't even know what to say. I am no longer a professor, and the walk with my personal effects from my office to the entrance of the university, with Director Greco beside me, was humiliating. Students watched, knowing something was going on, their faces a mixture of confusion and concern. We'd passed several that I knew, that I had mentored through the last few terms, and I had hoped would show a lot of promise, and that stung.

The whole time, though, I feared Emma would see me. And that would have burned even more.

Now, hours later, Emma is frozen on the stairs, and I don't know how to start. "Are you...Did you...?" What if she lost everything too?

Emma blinks, shaking her head clear. "You got fired?"

"Yes."

She takes a deep breath, and with fumbling fingers, she digs out the key to her apartment and lets us in. I hover by the door as she puts down her bag and strips off her jacket.

"What happened?" I ask.

Emma perches on the couch and tells me about being called into Greco's office and the conversation they had. Her hands fidget the whole time, tugging on her braid or picking at the seam of a throw pillow. I suck in my breath when she tells me she's lost the internship.

Her eyebrows furrow. "He didn't even ask me about you. He didn't mention your name other than to say that you were no longer with the school."

I scrape my palm against my beard. "No, he probably thought having less information would cover his ass. Minchia!" I pace away from Emma. Her apartment is not much bigger than the hallway, but having her here helps.

"What did they say when they fired you?"

"They said that they had explicit knowledge that I'd failed to disclose a previous relationship with you before the program started. If I had to guess, Vincente went to the director. He knew that I'd taken you home that night and he's—resentful of me right now. He suspected that something else was going on but doesn't have any proof, so the reason they gave me is the one they have the strongest argument for. I exhibited "unethical behavior" by failing to report our relationship." When the director had asked me if I had taken Emma home that night at the bar all those months ago, I couldn't lie.

"And my internship is gone. Just like that."

Greco is punishing Emma. He doesn't want to kick her out of the program, because graduation and placement rates matter too much, but he can punish her in other ways. "You got the internship, and that is a big deal. You will get another one."

Emma's fingers close around the pillow in a death grip. "I have to test again. Retake tests covering material I learned months ago. And now I have nine tests instead of six in the next few weeks. How am I going to study for all this?"

"I'll help you."

Emma's eyes squeeze shut, and she bites her lip. Anguish rolls over me in a wave when she opens her eyes and I can see that they are filled with tears. Angry tears, frustrated tears.

"Emma," I say, crouching down at her feet. "I am so sorry."

She sniffs, hurriedly rubbing her eyes before they can well over. "I'd like to be alone right now."

I hesitate. I feel like scum. Like the worst human on earth. Because of me, Emma, this beautiful woman who doesn't think she's light and bubbly and fun, is hurting and in pain. Worst, she's doubting herself.

We've been spending so much time together lately, and it feels simultaneously like it's been forever, and yet, just yesterday that I met her in a bar over glasses of wine.

Emma looks up at me, and while her gaze traces my face, her frown deepens, and I know that right now, she's thinking about what our relationship has cost her.

Because that's all I can think about right now too. Not even my own firing feels as unjust and sudden as Emma's punishment.

"Okay," I say, standing. "Just, if you need anything, call me." I'd come running. What else am I going to be doing?

I have nothing left.

41

———

Emma

I FEEL STUPID, HONESTLY. BAD FRIENDS WOULD SAY "I TOLD YOU so" when I tell them how badly we've fucked up.

But I have amazing friends. They listen with sympathy and understand that I have to cancel our weekend trip together, and then they ask how they can help me.

"I don't know," I say. "I have so much to do. It's overwhelming."

"We could come visit you instead of going to Amsterdam?" Jade suggests. "We'll stay out of your hair and bring you food and make sure you sleep."

"No, thanks. You should go have fun without me."

"What about just one of us?" Tessa asks. "I can bring work with me, and we can have a productivity retreat?"

"No, it's okay. I think it would just be distracting."

"Okay." She chews her lip. "How is Santo taking it?"

I think back to finding him waiting for me at the top of the stairs, how his eyes were wide and his hair ruffled. "Not well." I wonder if he's called Bell or talked to Vincente or if he's just stewing in his apartment next door in frustration and self-loathing. "He offered to help me, but I don't think I can handle being around him right now. He's lost his job, and it just feels...awful to see him. I can't picture him helping me study. It feels too much like rubbing salt in a wound." For both of us, I think.

As if reading my mind, Jade speaks up. "For you too. You lost a great opportunity. There will be more, but you are allowed to be mad."

"I am mad," I assure her. I'm mad at myself and Santo and the school and whoever reported Santo. But I try to push that emotion away, because who has the time? I have nine exams to prepare for.

I say goodbye to my friends, who give me lots of concerned looks and blow kisses through the screen. When we hang up, I grab my phone and reach out to someone who *can* help me study.

Half an hour later Shonda and I meet to tackle strategy at one of the big tables in the university's public spaces. She's brought Thai takeaway and together, while we're eating, I tell her I have to retake three tests.

"Does this have to do with Professor Offredi getting fired?" She looks up from her Pad Thai.

I nibble my lip. "Yeah."

She tilts her head, and her gaze sharpens. "Like, in the bad way or the good way? Just because he was a kickass teacher doesn't mean he wasn't a secret prick."

"Um...it was a mutual thing. I, uh...had fun."

Shonda stares at me before throwing her head back and cackling. "Damn, girl." She chuckles while picking a jalapeno out of her meal and then looks up at me through her lashes. "You two would be cute together. I kinda thought you liked him."

My cheeks heat. "Well, regardless, I have to finish the term and pass these tests and then apply for more internships."

"One step at a time," she says.

We crack open our books (figuratively) and block out scheduling times from now up to our exams. And then, with bellies full but a lot on our plates, we start with Supply Chain Management.

We're into our third block of studying and going over a section in our Negotiating class when Shonda leans over my laptop to look at the screen. "Why are you looking at triple bottom line stuff?"

"I'm just trying to refresh my memory. That's one of the tests I have to retake."

She settles back into her seat. "Just don't lose focus on what you're supposed to be studying."

When the hour is up, it's ten o'clock, and we're both yawning. "All right, I'm calling it. Do you want to meet here tomorrow right after classes?"

"Sure," I say. I don't pack up my stuff, but instead, open up some of the course videos for Business Analytics, the first term class I took with Santo.

"Are you going to stay here?"

"Yeah."

"Emma," she says, and her tone is gentle and filled with concern. "Don't forget you have to prioritize. Sleep is important."

"I know. But this was the first class, and it's been months. I feel like I've forgotten most of it, and these classes kind of build on each other, right?"

Shonda frowns. "I think you need to trust your memory more and take care of yourself."

"I'll be fine," I promise. "It's only a couple weeks."

With a sigh, Shonda says goodbye and heads home. I study for a few more hours, and this table is where I find myself spending all of my free time outside of class over the next two weeks. I pass my fourth term tests, but my grades are the lowest I've had all program. Shonda has an internship here in Rome, and she bullies me into continuing to meet her as often as I can; and she reviews the old class materials with me.

I don't see Santo at all. I get home late and go right to bed every night. I have no idea what he's doing, but I think if I was home to hear Oliver bark or the doors of the hallway opening and closing, I'd be thinking about Santo too much. I'm still upset, and even though he offered his help, I don't need it. Shonda is helping me, and that's enough.

42

Santo

THE KNOCK ON MY DOOR MID-AFTERNOON HAS ME LEAPING TO my feet, sending Zola scrambling and hissing up to her loft. Emma hasn't reached out, despite my offer to help her study, and I've been respecting her request for distance. I think she's had her tests by now, but I haven't heard anything from her, from Vincente, or from any of my former colleagues at the university.

When I open the door, though, it's not Emma but Bell on the other side. As soon as she'd heard about my firing, she'd come over to console me, but I hadn't talked to her in a few days.

"Not the person you were hoping for, I see," she says when she steps inside. Hearing her voice, Zola *merows* from the loft. After scratching Zola's chin, Bell takes her jacket off and drapes it over the arm of my couch before sitting in the corner. "How are you?"

I slump down next to her. "I was thinking about going out to Castel Gandolfo for a few weeks. Once Emma moves out for her internship, nothing is keeping me here. Except you," I quickly amend.

Bell faces me, propping her head up on her fist. "Have you talked to her?"

"No." Zola's head appears, her whiskers raised while she sniffs and considers whether Bell will give her more scratches. I flick my fingers to encourage her, but she turns away, rubbing her chin against the table and turning away from me, tail straight up in the air.

"Why not?"

I sigh and lean my head back. "I offered to help her study, and she hasn't reached out. Because of me, her opportunity is gone. And maybe her reputation. I don't know who knows what, and I think maybe it would be best to just not interfere."

Bell shifts and glares at me. "Do you love her?"

"I, ah…no. I don't love her." I close my eyes. "But I think I could. She lacks confidence in a lot of things, and when I look at her or talk to her, I think that I've found this undiscovered gem, that I see something other people can't see." I open my eyes and look at the closest thing I have to a daughter. "But she's leaving anyway, and she's angry and hurt."

"What about getting your job back?"

I scoff. "That will not happen."

Bell folds her arms, and her glare intensifies. "There was that case last year where the judge ruled in favor of the teacher getting his job back, claiming that they were in love, so it didn't matter that the student was seventeen and the teacher was forty-five."

I look at her, incredulous. "I am not a pedophile."

"I *know*," she says, exasperated. "If that horrible man was able to use a broken system to validate his relationship, then you can use a broken system to do the right thing without guilt. Your university doesn't even have a policy."

"How do you know?"

She wiggles her eyebrows. "I have my ways." I roll my head over to glare at her. "I called and asked. A woman in the human resources department was very helpful."

"Be that as it may, I don't want to fight to go back to a place I'm not wanted, and I don't want to make it harder on Emma."

"Well, then what's next?"

I grunt and sit forward, putting my head in my hands. "I don't know. How did I let this get so messy? How did I become my father?"

"Shut up. You are nothing like your father."

"People keep trying to tell me that, and I still don't think it's true."

Finally, Zola commits and jumps up on the couch, rubbing her face against Bell's proffered hand and, once again, pointing her ass at me. She really knows how to kick me when I'm down. Bell gathers Zola up and puts her in her lap. "Okay, so if you were your father, what would he do in this situation?"

"Give her a lot of money to go away, tank her career, and never speak of her again."

"And what's the opposite of that?"

"Give her no money, boost her career, and talk about her all the time?"

"Exactly."

"That makes no sense. The first one is done, the second one she doesn't want my help with, and who would I talk about her to?"

Bell shrugs. "She didn't want your help studying, but that doesn't mean she's going to refuse all help from you for all eternity. And who *should* you talk to about Emma?"

I think for a moment. "Her friends?"

Bell jostles Zola when she backhands my shoulder. "Santo! Help her find an internship."

"You think she would accept my help?"

"She'd be stupid not to. You know better than anyone what a leg up feels like. Talk her into it." She leans her shoulder against me. "You're very persuasive."

43

Emma

After my last retest, Shonda meets me at a local wine bar to celebrate. It's been a hectic time, and I am so relieved that it's over.

"To you, for kicking ass these past few weeks," Shonda proposes, lifting her glass.

"To it being done," I add.

We both sip the fruity house red we ordered. "How do you think this last one went?" she asks as we put our glasses down. This last test was for Innovation and Corporate Entrepreneurship.

"Better, I think. Professor Wang said she'd have my grade ready by noon tomorrow." Then I'll have a full transcript, the incompletes replaced by grades—assuming I passed this last test. Then I'll focus my energy on finding an internship. "I can't thank you enough, Shonda. Honestly, I couldn't have done it without you. Thanks for keeping me on track and keeping at it, even after your term was over."

"Yeah, about that." Shonda sets her glass down on the bar

top. Her eyes are on the stem of her wineglass as she rolls it around. "There's something I wanted to ask you."

"Okay," I say slowly.

"Look, I hope you aren't mad, but I was talking to my mom recently, and I told her about how we've been study-buddies together."

"Study-buddies?"

"I'm cute, I know." She flashes a grin at me. "Anyway, my mom is a psychologist, and I had kind of wondered if..." Shonda wrinkles her nose. "I wondered if there was something that she would recommend to help you. Aside from the schedule blocking and keeping a notebook on hand, the stuff you already do."

"Okay," I repeat.

"She said you could talk to a doctor about being tested for ADHD."

My eyebrows go up. "I don't have ADHD. I'm forty-two. When my kids were in school, we were taught to look for signs."

"Mom says it went undiagnosed in girls a lot because we don't often have the more obvious signs like hyperactivity. Or it could be a new thing. Perimenopause can cause more pronounced symptoms. And you have a lot of coping mechanisms you use already, so I'm not saying it's a problem for you. But ADHD after all this time is more likely than you might realize." She smiles at me. "Sorry, I sound like my mom. It doesn't have to mean anything. You're pretty great as it is. Otherwise, you wouldn't have made it here."

My brain starts spinning as I remember the scattered focus, the lost keys, all the way back to last summer when I missed a flight when I got confused about the dates. Could ADHD be the explanation for all of that?

"I...I'll think about it."

"Cool," Shonda says. There's a moment of silence between us before I turn and elbow her.

"Perimenopause? Really?"

She laughs. "Sorry." And then she changes the subject to something I'm even less excited to talk about. "Have you talked to Professor Offredi at all?"

I groan and slump down. I've been trying not to think about it, and my studies were a great distraction. "I haven't. I don't know what to say to him. Sorry I got you fired? I miss you?"

When Shonda doesn't answer, I look up at her. She gestures forward. "That sounds about right. Why not?"

"Because…because what happened was *awful*. You didn't see how distraught he looked. He loved his job and because of me, it was taken away from him. It's going to haunt me for a long time, I think." Every time I closed my eyes since that day, I've seen Santo waiting for me at the top of the stairs, and the guilt hits me hard.

"And yet he risked that job for you. He knew what he was getting into."

"That doesn't make it any better."

Shonda shrugged. "How about this: you might never see him again."

My heart clenches. That is true. Santo would move out because why would he stay in his apartment if he wasn't working for the university? He has his villa, he has Bell, and I am surprised he hasn't left already.

Before, when I thought about how I was leaving for my internship, I always knew I'd see Santo when I came back for the fall term and commencement. Now he won't be here.

I don't have to say anything; Shonda gives me a look of sympathy. "Sorry, girl."

We order another round, and I get Shonda talking about her first week at her internship. It is nice to hear about something going right, and I try to be a good friend and listen. After we drain our second glasses, we part ways, and I trudge back home.

It had been a sunny day, the kind that heralds spring, though still chilly. The sun had set while I had drinks with Shonda, though it was still early for dinner, at least in Italy.

At home, I shed my coat and checked my phone. There was discussion in my group chat with my friends about planning our next weekend together. Jade had been given a new work assignment that had her traveling, plus with Sara bouncing between Austin and London and Tessa frequently traveling from the Algarve to Paris, seeing each other once a month wasn't sounding so feasible anymore. And yet we hadn't canceled a weekend until my school fiasco.

That made me feel guilty too.

I am scrolling through the messages when Oliver barks next door.

I freeze, listening.

"Taci!" Eva shouts, and after a few more barks, Oliver simmers down.

I finally catch up—the front-running plan is for us to go to London—and type out a message—*I'll have to see what the career center says tomorrow. I don't think I can commit to anything right now.*—when Oliver barks again.

I spin in my seat, facing the wall between Eva's apartment and mine. Is Santo pleasuring himself? Oh my god, does he have a woman over?

I put my face in my hands, tears forming in my eyes. If I couldn't find an internship outside of Rome, or if I had to take a research position, was this what life was going to be like? Even if I did move, was a dog barking ever going to not make me think of Santo?

Oliver quiets. I put on some music and tried to think of anything other than what might be going on two doors down. I open my fridge and survey the contents, debating about what to cook for dinner. Nothing sounds good, so I close the fridge and open the pantry. I have some crackers and salami, which makes me think of dining in the kitchen of Santo's villa. I slam that door closed.

Oliver barks again. I can hear it, even over my music.

"Goddamnit Oliver!"

I stomp toward my door, anger and frustration driving me, though I'm not sure if I am going to yell at Eva or Santo.

I throw open the door and a *meow* greets me. I stare down at Zola, who blinks up and purrs.

When I make no move, she raises one paw, batting at the air, and *meows* again. When I bend down, she sits back on her haunches and lets me pick her up under her arms, pulling her into a cradle against my chest.

"Hi, Miss Zola," I say, tears clogging my throat. "What are you doing out here?" I glance at Santo's door, and there's a bottle of wine on the floor in front of it. I walk over and pick it up. It's a Prosecco, of course. When I stand, I notice there are envelopes taped to the door. Five envelopes, and they all have my name on the front in Santo's blocky handwriting.

I bend over to put the wine bottle down again, freeing up a hand to pull an envelope off the door. It's not sealed, so with Zola in the crook of my arm, I'm able to use both hands to open it. Zola ignores me jostling her around.

The envelope falls to the floor as I pull the two sheets of folded paper out. The top page is a bio printed off Sothebys' website. There's a blonde woman's headshot, and the text at the top reads:

DANETTE LÉVESQUE

SENIOR VICE PRESIDENT, LONDON

There are a few paragraphs detailing her background and highlighted is the part saying that Danette has an MBA from my university. Beneath that is a handwritten note from Santo.

Worked with me on Procurement research.

The second page is a printout of a job description for a three-month finance internship in Sothebys' London office.

I let the paper fall to the ground and pluck another envelope off the door. A student from two years ago who, like me, had Santo for a business fundamentals professor and now worked at Patek Philippe, the watch company, and an opening for a supply chain internship in Zurich. The next was merchandising at Mercedes' F1 team. Then a perfumer in Paris and a hotel chain based in Edinburgh.

I clutch Zola to my chest. What has Santo done?

It takes me a minute to raise my hand and knock once on the door. It opens immediately. Santo stands in the doorway, a hand bracing against the wall.

"I called some of my former students and asked around. You would still have to apply and interview, but I gathered some options for you. It's no more than the career center would have done for any other student."

I swallow. I have an appointment with the career center tomorrow. While most of the students find positions through the school, it's not a requirement. Some students reach out to companies on their own or apply through a network of International MBA universities.

Santo had done some legwork for me. He was giving me a nudge, trying to make up for our mistake.

"Thank you," I say.

Santo bends down to gather up the papers I've dropped, and instead of swapping his cat for them, he moves back and gestures me inside.

The door closes behind me, and I look around his apartment. His table is covered in books and papers, and I raise an eyebrow.

Santo rubs his hand across his beard. "I need an apartment with an office, I think. My previous place, the one you saw in October, had more space, but I gave it up because I had my office at the school, and I never used the extra rooms." His chuckle is dark.

"I'm sorry you lost your job."

Santo's gaze meets mine. "I know you are. But it's not your fault." He sighs, eyes shifting away before coming back to me. "Some days, I'm more angry at the university, and some days, I'm more angry at myself. But it's getting better."

"What will you do?" The internships on the door had been all over Europe, but none had been in Italy.

Santo folds his arms across his chest, leaning against the wall. "I was going to go to Castello and work on my book."

"You were? Past tense?"

A smile flickers across Santo's face, and he raises the stack of papers in his hands. "Every former student I talked to asked if I was going to consult more now. But one of them asked if I would consider joining a mentorship program. I've been pursuing both options, but my preference would be to go wherever you go. If you'll have me."

He's dead serious now, earnest as he watches my reaction. Zola *meows*, and I realize I'm squeezing her too tight. Gently, I let her jump to the floor where she raises her tail and rubs against Santo once before trotting up the stairs to her loft.

"What does that mean?"

"In my dreams, you get the internship that excites you the most. Wherever that takes you, I rent an apartment with enough room for the three of us. I'll finally finish my book. Maybe I'll consult, maybe I'll mentor, maybe I'll do nothing."

I give him a skeptical look.

"Unlikely," he allows. "But a possibility."

"You would make a great mentor," I add. "You should do that. But I have to come back here in the fall."

"Yes. That is why I will leave my options open."

"I was going to go back to Texas after graduation," I warn him.

Santo reaches out, tugging my braid. "By then, we will be

wildly in love with each other, and I'll follow wherever you go," he repeats. "If you'll have me."

I nod and throw my arms around Santo's neck. I might already be a little bit in love with him. No one has ever seen so much potential in me like he has.

Santo wraps his arms around my waist and pulls me in tight. We stand there, his hand gently stroking my back and me inhaling deeply, breathing Santo in. His embrace feels so good, and I love the dreams he has for our future.

When we pull apart, Santo grins at me. "Why don't we open the bottle and celebrate?"

EPILOGUE

Emma

Months later...

"Damn, this place is amazing," Jade says, walking into the kitchen of Santo's Castel Gandolfo villa.

"I know, right?" I grin as I close the fridge door. Santo lent us his villa for our weekend getaway. He's in Rome, unpacking our stuff and settling Zola into our new apartment, and I get to hang out with my friends before I report to the university on Monday to start a research project.

I have two months of research ahead of me, and then six weeks of the fall term, the last of my classes before graduation. My new ADHD prescription has helped, I think, but I'm nervous to see how it will work when I'm getting graded again. I liked my internship, though, and made new friends, and my boss told me to keep in touch about a full-time position.

In a few months, I'll have my MBA.

But for now, it's August, and it's sweltering in the city. It was a bad time to move from Edinburgh, where I'd done my internship. There, it was downright chilly and overcast. It was a very different summer than I was used to.

I'd had a great time, though. Santo and I had rented a three-bedroom apartment near the corporate offices of Thistle & Croft Hospitality, a conglomerate that owned several luxury brands of boutique hotels in the British Isles. Santo was almost done with his book, and he'd enjoyed connecting with former students in the area.

The worst part was the accents. I'd hoped that by picking a location where English was spoken, I would fit in better, but the Scottish accent made socializing challenging. I was glad to have Santo with me.

Speaking of, I grab my phone and text Santo while Jade grabs a glass of wine and joins Tessa and Sara out on the terrace.

EMMA

We made it to the villa. Everything looks great.

SANTO

I'm glad. The rental car did okay?

EMMA

Yeah. Getting out of the airport was a nightmare, but we survived.

SANTO

Have a great weekend. Tell everyone hi. Love you and see you Sunday.

EMMA

Love you too.

I step outside just in time. The sun is down over the hills, and the breeze is blowing, finally cooling the air and making it the perfect temperature.

"It's boring," Sara says. "The same guy wins every time. And the tickets are so expensive, but Chris wants to go."

"Go to what?" I ask.

"The Formula 1 race in October. It's in Austin."

"We've been watching," Tessa says. "Luc roots for Alpine, the French team, of course. But he also likes an underdog." Here in Italy, Ferrari is the second religion. Santo, who prefers to watch soccer, still follows.

"Is there a particular reason Chris wants to go to the one in Austin and not one of the ones in Europe?" I ask Sara. "You spend half your time here."

Sara and Chris spent most of winter in Austin leading up to South by Southwest, and then spent most of spring in London while Chris did some work in recording studios. He missed his band, who had broken up last year, but he was writing more songs than ever.

"He wants to do that, too. But tickets to the UK races are even harder to get."

"Even for a rock star like Chris?" I tease.

Sara grins. "Even for him."

The three of us glance at Jade. She hasn't said anything since I came out here, and her mind is elsewhere—she stares off into the distance, eyes unfocused, not seeing the sunset or the cyprus trees. My eyebrows draw together. It's not like Jade to be melancholy, though I know she's under a lot of stress lately. She's been traveling for work a lot more, giving presentations and meeting the people who use the medical hair products she develops.

"Jade?" Sara calls.

She startles. "What?"

Tessa gives her a concerned look. "Where were you?"

"Sorry." Jade shakes her head. "I wasn't paying attention. What were you saying?"

"Is this about your work?" Sara asks. "Are you doing okay?" Jade's work is near and dear to her heart, but it has to be tough seeing cancer patients more often when Jade is used to managing a team of scientists and working with data.

"Work is okay." She bites her lip. "It's not work related, really. Well, it is, but it isn't."

My frown deepens.

"Okay, you better tell us before Emma goes mama-bear on you," Tessa jokes. "Seriously, what's going on?"

Jade's gaze goes unfocused again. "I saw Carlos coming out of his hotel room with a woman."

Carlos works for the same company Jade does, and they've been traveling together. He's on the marketing side and speaks several languages, so he translates the presentations and questions from patients. They don't get along very well, and Jade hates having to travel with him.

"I mean, I don't care if he's seeing anyone," she continues. "But it hasn't come up at all, and isn't that weird? She was young, too, maybe in her thirties. I'm just surprised, that's all."

"Did you ask him about her?" I ask.

"No." It's petulant, and then Jade throws back her head. "Argh! Why is he so hard to talk to?"

Jade has always been straightforward, and when she first started her position in Madrid, she asked Carlos out. He said no and then was weird about it.

"If it weren't for these presentations, everything would be fine. He's in a different department. We hardly ever saw each other. Why can't I have a different translator? Why?" She ends on a wail, throwing her head back. She brought up concerns when her boss gave her the assignment, but Carlos was the best for the job—as was Jade.

"Sorry, sweetie," Tessa says, bending forward to pat her knee. "It's only temporary."

The four of us go quiet. Jade's time in Madrid is almost up. She was the first one to convince us to come here, and now she'll be the first to leave. It's been a topic of conversation between us a lot lately.

Tessa and Luc are moving in together in Paris. Sara and

Chris plan to eventually move to London full-time. I still have a few months left in my MBA program, and after that, Santo and I will move to Austin.

Our monthly visits will be over. Flying around Europe is a lot easier than flying across an ocean, and we aren't sure how it's going to work out. Yearly visits? Who knows.

At least we have one thing to look forward to: Sara and Chris's wedding, which is happening next year.

"And on that note," Jade says. "Can we finally go to Monaco?"

That breaks the tension with eye rolls and laughter. We decide that yes, since next month is our last weekend together before Jade moves back, we will finally go to Monaco.

We make plans for the next day, too—things I didn't do on my last trip here because I was too busy having sex with Santo. We'll visit the Pontifical Villas and Gardens, go for a swim in Lake Albano, and dine at a restaurant Santo recommended, a gift certificate for it in my wallet as a special treat from him.

For now, though, I sip my Prosecco and sneak a peek at my phone. There's a selfie from Santo of him on the couch with Zola on his chest with the caption, *Miss you.*

THE END

ACKNOWLEDGMENTS

With this series, I've strived to portray four women with different shapes and sizes and different feelings about their bodies. My own body has been through wild changes, especially through the ages of seventeen to twenty-two. That time was pretty unhealthy for me, physically, but I find now, as a nearly forty-year-old woman, it's harder mentally. Writing books is cathartic for me, and I hope that, if you need it, you find a book that is cathartic for you.

Thank you to my early readers, Sara Whitney and Cara Dion, and my beta readers, Lainey Davis, Elise Kennedy, and Serena Bell.

My friend Fabio was an extremely helpful consultant to me for both medical subjects and Italian language advice.

Thank you to my proofreader, Lisa Matsumura, and to Kate Mahon for the amazing cover.

And as always, a big thank you to my husband, who encouraged me so much from day one, and my parents, all five of them, who supported this book in one way or another.

ABOUT LIZ ALDEN

Liz Alden is a digital nomad. Most of the time, she's on her sailboat, but sometimes she's in Texas. She knows exactly how big the world is—having sailed around it—and exactly how small it is, having bumped into friends worldwide. She's been a dishwasher, an engineer, a CEO, and occasionally gets paid to write or sail.

Follow Liz:
Instagram | Facebook | X | LizAlden.com